“Her Christmas Detective”

The Gingerbread Inn #3

By Laura Ann

This is a work of fiction. Similarities to real people, places, or events are entirely coincidental.

HER CHRISTMAS DETECTIVE

First edition. December 10, 2020.

Written by Laura Ann.

DEDICATION

To my mother.
Your support is immeasurable.

ACKNOWLEDGEMENTS

No author works alone. Thank you, Brenda.
You make it Christmas every time
I get a new cover. And thank you to my Beta Team.
Truly, your help with my stories is immeasurable.

CHAPTER 1

Bella rushed down the hallway of the Cliffside Bed and Breakfast, otherwise known to the locals as the Gingerbread Inn. It was her grandmother's inn and Bella was thrilled to be working at it for the holiday season. *Well…mostly thrilled.*

She had graduated over a year ago with her degree in journalism and had been trying to take the world by storm ever since. However, the fact that she struggled to get her pieces picked up by anyone showed she still had more work to do.

So when Grandma Claire had fallen and broken her hip, but wanted to keep the inn open for Christmas, Bella and her favorite two cousins, Hope and Emory, had come running to help.

And right now, the running was literal. Strange things had been happening at the inn and Sheriff Davidson, a man that Bella was positive had a crush on her grandmother, had called in a detective to help. They were supposed to be meeting with said detective and Bella was late…as usual.

For someone who tried hard to be on top of all the news all the time, she had a knack for losing track of the clock and right now, it was about to cost her.

"Where's Bella?"

The words came from the large sitting room just ahead. Putting on a burst of speed, she rushed through the doors. "Coming!" Bella held in her laughter. *Talk about a grand entrance.* She'd never been afraid of the limelight, unlike her cousins, and sometimes she reveled in it. What good was a journalist who was afraid of being on the front lines?

As she skidded into the ballroom, Bella found herself stumbling to a stop, her jaw falling open. Standing in the midst of her family and friends was a stranger. A very handsome stranger.

He was tall and well built, towering over her small five-foot-two stature. His broad shoulders showed his time spent in the gym, while his perfectly styled blond hair told her he also spent time in front of the mirror. *Oh, my...* His jaw was strong and square and a perfect complement to the rest of his rugged masculinity. "Well, hello..." Bella purred. *Who is this and how can I get to know him?*

"You must be Isabella," the man said smoothly, his dark eyes focused on her.

"I must be, indeed," she said, making sure her hips were swinging as she finished walking into the room. "And you are?"

"Detective Gordon." He smiled and Bella's heart fluttered. "Henry Gordon. But everyone calls me Hank."

Bella brushed aside the nickname. His real name had a much more pleasant ring to it. "Nice to meet you, Henry." Bella held out her hand and gave him a firm shake. She might be completely bowled over by his looks, but she wasn't about to come off as weak. That wasn't her style at all, and any man who wanted a damsel in distress needed to look elsewhere.

Mrs. Harrison sighed loudly from across the room. "Where is the sheriff? Is he not coming?"

Henry spun away from Bella and turned to face the woman who was a guest at the inn. It was because of her missing ring that Detective Gordon had been called in the first place. "He should be here shortly," Henry explained. "He had a call in town he needed to finish."

While his back was turned, Bella turned to Hope and lifted her left hand, pointing at the ring finger. "He's not wearing a ring!" she mouthed excitedly, having checked it out when they shook hands.

Hope smiled and nodded. "Go for it!" she mouthed back.

Bella bounced on her toes, turning back to the detective. She could hear Antony, Mrs. Harrison's son and a local baker, holding back laughter, as well as Enoch, the full-time handyman at Gingerbread Inn.

Detective Gordon glanced over his shoulder at her, his eyes dark and intense, and Bella gave him her best smile. There must have been something in the air at Gingerbread Inn this year, because Bella had noticed that her two cousins were having similar reactions to the two other men in the room.

Hope and Enoch were practically joined at the hip, and even though Emory and Antony had begun their relationship by fighting like cats and dogs, they were now standing awfully close for people who didn't get along.

Maybe now it's my turn, Bella mused. She pursed her lips with a grin as the detective turned back to Mrs. Harrison. *I certainly wouldn't mind spending a little time with a hunky detective. Merry Christmas to me!*

"Why don't we go around and you can all tell me your side of things, hm?" Detective Gordon said calmly to Mrs. Harrison. "Bill," he said, referring to Sheriff Davidson, "has heard all this before, so when he gets here we can jump into the thick of it."

Mrs Harrison sighed dramatically, then jumped into her story. "I brought a ring with me on this trip, one that was very special." She looked forlornly down at her empty finger and Bella almost felt sorry for her. If the woman hadn't been accusing Hope, who was working as the inn's housekeeper, of being the thief, Bella might actually believe all the drama. "I never go anywhere without it," Mrs. Harrison said softly.

"When did you last see it?" Henry asked, pulling out his phone and punching notes into an app.

"The night before it was taken, so two days ago." She sniffed. "I took it off, put it in the jewelry box I brought with me, and went to bed."

Who brings a jewelry box with them on vacation? Bella scoffed inwardly and shook her head. Despite her disbelief, she pulled out her phone and started to take her own notes. Something big was happening at Gingerbread Inn, and Bella was going to get to the bottom of it.

Although she loved her grandmother and would never regret helping out, running the front desk was far from exciting. Bella loved adventure. She liked to be in on the action. In fact, she preferred to be the one doing the action!

"Who all has been in your room since you were here?" Detective Gordon pressed.

Bella froze, her stylus stuck above her screen. This was where things might get sticky, and the decision as to whether or not she would get to know Henry better was right now. The rest of the group already knew that Mrs. Harrison was convinced Hope, the sweetest of all the sweet people in the world, had taken the ring.

"Only housekeeping!" Mrs. Harrison cried. "I have already said all this! It had to be her!"

The detective glanced toward Hope, then back to Mrs. Harrison without saying anything.

Bella narrowed her eyes, trying to read his body language. *Does he believe her? He isn't pressing Hope about anything.*

"Is there a possibility that someone else could have come in? You said you went right to bed. So it disappeared while you were sleeping?"

Mrs. Harrison fluffed her hair. "I left the room only momentarily," she admitted, her Italian accent weaker as she calmed down. "I wished to read for a few minutes before going to sleep, so I walked to the library."

Now we're getting somewhere...

"Is it possible someone else went in your room during that time?" Hank asked. "Did you leave the door unlocked?"

Mrs. Harrison shook her head. "I had my key with me, so no one could have gotten in unless they had one themselves." She raised an eyebrow. "Like a housekeeper."

Or maybe not.

HANK WAS HAVING A TERRIBLE time keeping his mind on Mrs. Harrison's testimony. One of the most adorable women he'd ever seen was off to the side of the room, bouncing on her toes and punching something into her phone. *Bill said she's a journalist and a spitfire.* He started to chuckle, then forced it to stop when Mrs. Harrison gave him an odd look. *I think spitfire might be an understatement, if her bold way of greeting me is any indication.*

Bella's dramatic entrance into the ballroom had certainly been eye-catching, but the long, strawberry blonde hair and bright blue eyes had kept his attention well past her arrival. She had a pixie-like face, with a small smattering of freckles across her nose. It made her look young, but her demeanor said otherwise.

She looked vibrant and full of life. Plus, those baby blues sparkled as if she held secrets...and Hank found himself wanting to figure them out.

"Aren't you going to arrest her?"

Hank blinked several times, pulling his mind from the beautiful woman to his left. "Sorry, Mrs. Harrison. We don't arrest people on hearsay." *Not to mention Bill said Hope wouldn't harm a fly, and unless she's the world's best actress, her frightened look tells me Bill is right.*

She hmphed, but Hank moved on.

"I will have to investigate everything you've told me, and then we'll move on from there." He stood, pocketing his phone. "I'll pull Hope aside and ask her some questions in a bit."

"Do you have any enemies?"

Hank turned to see Bella walking up to him and Mrs. Harrison. He frowned as he watched her. *What's she doing?*

"Enemies?" Mrs. Harrison balked. "I am a guest here," she said, her accent becoming stronger as she grew upset. "Who would I have as an enemy?"

Bella stopped by Hank's side, a stylus poised above her phone. "You never know, Mrs. Harrison. Have you spoken to anyone in town? Have you noticed that you're being followed? Has anyone made you feel unsafe during your trips to town?"

"What is this?" Mrs. Harrison asked, leaning away as if that would protect her from the rapid-fire questions.

"What indeed," Hank murmured. He gave Mrs. Harrison a polite, if fake, smile and gently took the interrogator's elbow. "Would you excuse us for a minute?" he said to Mrs. Harrison before leading Bella away. He walked her to the far side of the room and swung her into the corner as gently as he could through his frustration. "What do you think you are doing?" he asked. He fought to keep his tone low.

She looked up at him with wide, innocent eyes. "What do you mean?"

Hank squeezed his eyes shut and took a deep breath. This woman was beautifully distracting, but he was seeing why Bill said she might be trouble. "I mean...why are you interrogating Mrs. Harrison?"

Bella kept eye contact with them while slipping her phone into her back pocket, then she put her hands on her hips. "Why aren't you?"

He jerked back. "I did."

"No, you didn't," Bella argued. "You asked a couple of questions. You definitely didn't *interrogate* her. Interrogation involves asking things in a formal or aggressive manner." She smirked as if she'd won.

"I hate to disappoint you, Ms. Wood," he said, "but I've found you will always get more information with honey rather than vinegar." He smirked back. "So while I might not have been as aggressive as you wanted me to be, I got the information I needed without angering or scaring her." He folded his arms over his own chest. "That's a win-win in my book."

Bella rolled her eyes. "But how do you know that there isn't more to it? You need to put pressure on her...try and get her to crack and admit she just misplaced the ring." Her eyes widened. "OR!" She stepped closer to him, her citrusy scent overwhelming his senses. "Maybe she sold the ring and doesn't want her son to know."

Hank shook his head, completely dumbfounded by her wild ideas. "Tell me, Ms Wood. Just why would she sell an important family heirloom?"

She put her hands out, palm up. "The money, of course. Isn't that what everyone wants?"

"I don't think money is a problem for her," he pointed out.

Bella pointed a finger at him. "So she says."

"And so does her son," Hank replied. He straightened, cutting off their private conversation. Being stuck in the corner with her was starting to feel a little too intimate...making his mind wander to paths like dinners and holding hands, which would eventually lead to things like cuddling and kissing. He shook his head. *Keep it professional, Hank. You're here for a job.*

Bella squished her lips up, nearly touching her nose with the pout. "Fine. But I still think she's hiding something."

Hank couldn't help but chuckle. "I think your journalism degree is messing with your head." As soon as the words slipped out, he knew he shouldn't have said it. Not only was it not exactly kind, but it lit a fire under Bella that had him worried. And he barely knew her.

"Why?" she asked, her voice low and deadly. "Because journalists are all about sensationalizing everything? Because we would do anything to sell a headline?" She stepped into his space, poking him in the chest. "Or is it because I'm a *woman* journalist? Maybe we women just have more active imaginations? Am I too weak to see the truth for what it is?"

Hank finally held up his hands in surrender. "You'll have to forgive me, Ms. Woods. I let that slip out without thinking."

"But you *were* thinking it, and that's telling," she shot back.

Hank's shoulders drooped. "You're right," he admitted. "And it was wrong of me. You just seem really...eager...and I had an uncharitable thought. I shouldn't have said it, let alone thought it." He stuck out his hand. "Truce? Can we start over?"

She narrowed her eyes at him, but finally took his hand.

Hank tightened his grip and pulled her slightly closer. "And just so we're clear. You being a woman has nothing to do with anything. I know women on the force who would beat me up for thinking otherwise."

Her delightfully soft-looking lips twitched at his comment. "Glad to hear it." She pulled her hand out of his and stepped back, running a hand down her hair. "So...Emory made donuts this morning. If we're careful, we could sneak a couple and compare notes?"

Her grin was entirely too alluring and Hank found himself grinning back automatically. "Actually, I doubt we have to sneak at all. She offered me one earlier, before you arrived."

Bella gave a jerk of her head. "Dang. I miss all the good stuff. What kind of journalist does that make me?"

Hank chuckled. "A normal one, I suspect."

She sighed and rolled her eyes. "Come on, Sherlock. I'll show you where my cousin keeps her sweets."

Hank dutifully followed along, thinking that Bella, despite her enthusiasm, might prove to be sweeter than any donut. *Hopefully this case will be over quickly so I can take a little time to get to know this stunning woman before she goes back home.*

CHAPTER 2

Bella led Hank into the kitchen, heading straight for the cupboard she knew Emory kept the leftover pastries in. Bella's cousin was an incredible baker and had slid seamlessly into the role as the kitchen manager at the inn. Bella opened the cupboard and reached up, but found herself slightly too short to reach what she wanted. Grunting in frustration, she bounced on her toes and was able to pull the Tupperware container out just to the edge of the shelf.

"Here. Let me." Henry's smooth baritone came from close behind Bella, but it was the warmth of his presence that had her jumping slightly.

"Oh!" she squeaked. Taking a deep breath, she forced her body to calm down. *Knock it off,* she scolded internally. *You've dealt with attractive men before.*

His large arm reached over her head, retrieving the storage container, then he stepped back and offered it to her.

"Thanks," Bella said, boldly giving him a wink. She held back a laugh at his surprised look. She absolutely loved putting people off balance. "I'll just warm a few of these up." She opened another cupboard, grabbing a plate, then put a few of Emory's delectable apple cider donuts on it. After a few seconds in the microwave, they were wafting an irresistible scent that had Bella's mouth watering.

"I have to admit those smell good," Hank said, his hands on his hips. "Emory might be everything Bill said she was."

A small pang of jealousy hit Bella, but she pushed it away. *If he was interested in Emory, he wouldn't be in here with me. Plus, Antony might have something to say about it.* However, the fact that she was even feeling jealousy at all let Bella know that she was unusually attracted to this man. *I better slow myself down, or he's gonna think I'm some crazy stalker chick, instead of a cool-headed journalist.* "Oh, she is," Bella said, walking away from him with the goodies. "And she's also very picky about who she lets in her kitchen, so if you don't want to see her cleaver skills first-hand, I'd recommend heading to the dining room with me."

Henry chuckled and followed her just like she'd asked. "Are you saying your cousin is dangerous?"

"Nope." Bella popped the 'p' at the end of the word. "But she is scary when she wants to be." Bella set the plate at the table and sat down. "I don't mess with her...ever. You never know when she'll cut off your carb intake."

"So noted." Henry took the chair across from her.

"Napkins!" Bella jumped up and ran to the sideboard, grabbing a stack. She smiled as she sat back down. "You'll end up with cinnamon and sugar all over your fingers by the time you're done."

"The kid inside of me says I should just lick it off," Henry teased. "The adult in me says I've been taught better manners than that."

Bella laughed. "It sounds to me like you had a good childhood."

"The best."

She waited while he took a donut and groaned after the first bite. "So what made you want to become a detective then?"

Henry put up a finger while he finished off the donut. "Sorry. I couldn't make myself stop," he said sheepishly. "Bill was right. Your cousin is an angel in the kitchen."

The jealousy tried to rise to the surface again, but Bella refused to listen. "She is." Bella nodded. "No one else can handle a treat like she can." Bella made a face. "Although, I've heard Antony's bakery is pretty amazing."

Henry nodded slowly. "Bill said that as well. Antony's apparently quite the bread baker, as well as being an award-winning cake decorator."

Bella's eyebrows shot up. "Wow. I didn't know that." She pulled out her phone. "Okay. We really need to swap notes, because you've done more research than I have."

Henry's eyes narrowed. "What exactly is your plan here, Ms. Woods?"

She gave him a look. "I keep ignoring it, but you calling me Ms. Woods drives me crazy. I'm Bella. Or Isabella if you want to be formal, but definitely *not* Ms. Woods."

Henry leaned back in his chair and folded his arms over his chest. "Okay...Bella. But I ask again, what is your plan?"

"I'm not sure I follow."

He tilted his head. "Are you trying to write an article about this? Trying to hit a headline in this sleepy town? Why are you so set on getting to the bottom of this situation?"

The tiny amount of jealousy that Bella had been feeling was gone in a flash. In its place was the anger from earlier. She copied his stance, leaning back and folding her arms. "I don't really see why I need to defend my interest to you."

"And I don't see why I should be swapping information with a civilian."

Bella rolled her eyes and leaned her elbows onto the table. "Okay...look. Anything that involves my family involves me. This place is my grandmother's pride and joy, and something funky is going on here. We've had tools moved. Garden tools left on the lawn. Food is missing. Like full-on pies," she said, raising her eyebrows for emphasis. "Although I don't know that that bothered Emory as much as the stolen French candy did."

"Bill told me most of those things," Henry said, still watching her carefully. "Although, it's clear he doesn't even know the half of it."

"You want to know the worst part?" Bella pursed her lips. "On top of all the strange stuff, we've got a cousin, one that Emory, Hope, and I didn't even know about, and his family is trying to sue for the inn. He simply showed up on the doorstep and declared that Grandma was incompetent." Bella blew out a raspberry. "It's ridiculous. We didn't even know we had cousins..." she frowned, "second cousins?" Bella shook her head. "Whatever they are, we didn't even know they existed. And now they're trying to take away our inheritance."

Hank sighed and pushed a hand through his hair. "Yeah...Bill mentioned that too, but I set it aside. The reason I was brought in was because a ring was stolen. Everything else has some kind of logical explanation." He held up his hand when Bella tried to interrupt and she snapped her mouth shut. "Let me rephrase that. Everything else *could* have a logical explanation. A stolen ring is a little more serious."

"*If* it was stolen," Bella pointed out. "I mean...it could have been misplaced. So there's a possible explanation for that as well, if you want to get technical."

Henry nodded. "I'll give you that, though the chances of it are less."

Bella shrugged. "Maybe."

"You still think Mrs. Harrison is lying?"

Bella shrugged again. "Not necessarily. But the woman obviously loves to make a scene. You should have seen the wailing that went on when she found it gone."

Henry chuckled. "That bad?"

"Like Biblical proportions bad," Bella said in a serious tone. She was enjoying this. Maybe not as much as she had hoped, but Hank was proving to be down to earth and intelligent, if not a little stubborn. Now she just needed to convince him that she had a right to be here just as much as he did.

Henry's smile grew. "Let's hope no one posts it on social media."

Bella snapped her fingers. "I knew I forgot something."

He laughed again. "Okay... Your explanation is good, but you're forgetting one thing."

"What's that?"

Henry gave her a serious look. "It's wonderful that you want to help your family and clear your cousin's name. But you're not trained for this sort of thing. In fact," he leaned onto the table, "you're more likely to be a hindrance than an asset. Don't you think you should let the professionals handle this?"

Oh no, he didn't... Bella sat up straight and gave him her best fake smile. "How nice. Your opinion has been noted." She stood up. "Thank you for the time, Detective Gordon. I'm sure I'll be seeing you around."

CRAP. CRAP. CRAP. Hank watched the upset woman walk out of the dining room. Now the question was whether or not he should go after her. With as nosy as she seemed to be, she might actually have information that would be helpful and save him some time.

On the other hand, he wasn't sure having an attractive woman following him around during a case would be a good idea, even if this was something rather small. He'd only come because he owed Bill a favor. Someone like Bella hadn't been on his radar, though.

She was intriguing, and Hank wouldn't mind getting to know her better, but he also had a job to do. Was it feasible to think he could hold off on his attraction until this was settled? "It's not like a missing ring is a big case," he muttered as he stood from the table. He picked up the plate to take back to the kitchen. "It'll probably be over quickly, and then if I want to ask her out, I can."

He nodded, firming his resolve. Work first, then play. *If it's not too late. She was pretty ticked.* Hank opened the door to the kitchen, women's voices reaching his ears.

"Can you believe that Neanderthal?" Bella complained to her cousin, who seemed busy at the oven. Bella was pacing, her silky hair blowing behind her as she paced. "Let the professionals handle this," Bella said in a tight, snippy voice. "As if eating donuts on the job is professional. Ha!"

"I'm no expert at voice types, but I'm pretty sure I don't sound like that." Hank raised an eyebrow, slightly amused and slightly frustrated at Bella's scene. When she spun with a gasp, he had to hold back laughter. She had had no idea he would hear her comments, and it was clear she was regretting them.

"Sorry, Detective," Emory said from her place at the stove. "Bella has no filter." She smiled over at him. "But we love her anyway."

"Gee, thanks," Bella grumbled.

Emory smiled over her shoulder, then went back to work, completely ignoring the two other people in the room.

Hank fought the desire to shift his weight from one side to the other. It was awkward to have an audience, no matter how much she was ignoring them, and he wasn't really sure what to do about Bella. It was clear she wasn't going to take his suggestion lying down, and he really didn't want her snooping where she shouldn't.

"Have anything to say for yourself, Detective?" Bella asked, her arms akimbo.

"Me?" Hank jerked back a little. "I wasn't the one cursing people to high heaven."

She rolled her eyes. "I wasn't cursing anyone. I was upset that you're treating me like a little kid."

Hank had no control over his eyes as they flitted from her face to her toes and back. "I'm fully aware you're not a little child," he said, his voice having gone slightly husky. *Could you be any more obvious?* He wanted to punch himself. He was acting ridiculous.

Bella's cheeks turned a light shade of pink and Hank chuckled. He hadn't thought she would be the type to blush.

Bella brushed her hair over her shoulder and stuck her chin in the air, a defiant look if Hank had ever seen one. "Whether you think that or not, you're treating me as fragile. Which I'm not. I'm headed into crime reporting, and this is exactly the type of thing I want to do."

"You want to report on stolen rings?"

Bella threw her hands in the air. "It's a starting point, isn't it? A crime was committed. I've done some sleuthing, and I want to be a part of the solution." She put her hands back on her hips and rapidly tapped her toe. "Now...are you willing to work with me or not?"

Hank sighed and pinched the bridge of his nose. "While I realize a stolen ring is a fairly small crime, there's still a chance of running into a criminal." He looked at her sternly. "What if you get caught in the middle of something? What kind of law enforcement officer would I be if I let that happen?"

Bella's shoulders fell. "I get it, Detective. I do. But this is what I've been working for. A mystery, no matter how small, is like a gift from heaven right now. It's exactly what I need."

"Why do I get the feeling that you'll keep doing what you're doing whether or not you have my permission?" Hank shook his head. He'd seen people like her. Eager to be involved and untrained. It usually meant they'd watched far too many episodes of CSI as a kid, and it always made for a messy case.

She grinned at him. "Because you're smart enough to read between the lines."

"Don't try to butter me up."

Emory and Bella both laughed. Hank shifted when he was reminded they weren't alone. The other woman was so quiet, he'd forgotten they had an audience.

"So...are you willing to share information or not?" Bella asked in a far too enticing manner.

Hank was still and silent. He didn't like it. Yes, he wanted to spend time with her, but not like this. Not when he was working. There were too many variables. Too many ways for things to go wrong or for her to do something that would jeopardize the case. A stolen ring might be a small case, but he was still going to take it seriously. It's what had gotten him to the job of detective at his age, and he wasn't going to drop the ball now.

"I'll even let you take me to dinner, if you agree," she teased.

Hank burst out laughing. "Let me get this straight. If I agree to share info, you'll let *me* take *you* to dinner?"

She smirked. "That's the price to work with a *professional* like myself."

Hank shook his head slowly. She was gutsy. And he liked it far too much. He glanced at his watch. "I need to get to the station. I'll pick you up tomorrow night at seven?"

Bella's entire body tightened, and he could see she was holding something in, but he wasn't sure if it was a cry of triumph or a groan of disdain. "Seven. Got it."

I'm probably going to regret this. With a nod to each woman in turn, he set down the plate of donuts and marched out of the room. He was only halfway through the ballroom when he heard a screech his sisters would make when they were excited, and dang if it didn't bring a smile to his face.

CHAPTER 3

Bella pursed her lips in the mirror and finished putting her lip gloss on with a flair. She grinned at herself when she was done. While she knew she wasn't model worthy, she wasn't usually upset about the way she looked. She was compact, but had a nice figure, and her strawberry blonde hair had always been an asset. The only thing that really bothered her was the freckles across her nose. They made her look younger than she was, and that was frustrating in her field.

"No sultry, come-hither looks from this baby face," she muttered as she cleaned up her make-up supplies and stuffed everything back in the drawer of her bathroom. She shrugged to herself as she grabbed her heels. "Maybe small-town detectives won't care about that."

The doorbell rang in the background and Bella gasped. "Darn it. Always late." She finished tumbling into her shoes, grabbed her coat, and rushed out the door of her suite, only to come back a moment later to grab her purse. It had her notebook in it, which she would need not only to take notes, but to share as well.

Muttering under her breath, she snagged her heel on the carpet before making it to the staircase, nearly flinging herself down them. Catching herself on the banister, she forced herself to take a deep breath. "Cool...smooth...you're a professional. Nothing ruffles your feathers." She held her chin aloft. "You're a journalist."

Slowing down in order to create the entrance she wanted, Bella walked as casually yet sexily as she could. She desperately wanted to use this time at the inn to be seen as the woman she was, *not* as some wanna-be who couldn't hold down a serious job. Going out with someone as rugged and handsome as Hank should help her pull off that image even more.

She sucked in a quiet breath when the detective came into view. He was wearing dress pants and a long-sleeved, button-up shirt that showed off his shoulders and broad chest a little too well. He was currently speaking to Hope in the foyer. The sleeves were rolled up to his elbows as if he'd come straight from work. The tie at his neck was loose and with today's styles, Bella knew that could go either way.

Her heart sank just a little. *Maybe he really is just viewing this as a business meeting. Did he not put any effort into what he looked like?* She suddenly felt very foolish over the time she'd spent putting her hair in curls and creating the perfect eyeliner effect. Apparently Mr. Henry Gordon, Detective Extraordinaire, wasn't even going to notice.

She brought her eyes up from her feet and nearly stumbled again when she met his dark stare. They were in such contrast to his golden, blond hair. And right now, they were watching her as if he hadn't eaten in a week.

A little thrill went up her spine as she finished descending the stairs. "Hello, Detective," she said in a smooth voice. At least she hoped it was smooth. It had left a little tickle in her throat and Bella was fighting hard to keep from coughing. It would ruin the entire image.

"Isabella," Hank said, his voice slightly husky. "You look amazing."

She smiled and stood a little taller under his praise. "Why, thank you." She purposefully looked him over from head to toe. "You're not so bad yourself." *There. Not lying. I mean, he IS super studly, but not exactly put together either.*

He chuckled. "You'll have to forgive the way I look. I got stuck doing paperwork and didn't have time to go home."

Bella shrugged. "No biggie."

"Don't forget your coat," Hope said softly from where she stood, waiting quietly near the door.

Henry reached out and took the coat that was hanging on Bella's arm. "Let me help you."

Bella was delighted with his gentlemanly assistance and slipped her arms through the sleeves. It wasn't the warmest coat she owned, but she'd be darned if she was going to show up in a puffy, no figure-flattering outfit in front of Henry Gordon.

He rested his hands on her shoulders. "You sure you'll be warm enough?"

"Yep," she chirped and began to walk toward the door. "Ready?"

Henry rushed up and held the door open for her. "After you."

Bella couldn't stop smiling. Gentlemen were few and far between in the big city and she was loving Henry's manners. *Maybe small-town life isn't going to be as boring as I feared.*

He held her door getting into the car and again at the restaurant. "Hope you like seafood," Henry said as they settled into their private booth.

Bella laughed. "Is there any other kind of food in a town right on the coast?"

"I heard there's an Italian place down the road."

She brushed him off. "We're right on the ocean. There's no better place to eat seafood. So I'm good."

Henry grinned at her and then put his focus on his own menu. For several minutes they were quiet and Bella quickly grew restless. Her leg was bouncing under the table and she had to put a hand on her knee to make it stop. She was afraid it would start shaking the table soon.

After they ordered and the menus were taken away, there was an awkward silence.

"So..." Henry folded his hands together on the table top. "You said you had information for me."

That sinking feeling in Bella's gut hit her again. She had hoped his reaction to her outfit meant this really was a date, but now he was all business again. *That's what professionals do,* she reminded herself. *Quit whining and deal with it.* Despite her firm scolding, Bella found herself disappointed. While she wanted to use this as a chance to progress as a reporter, she also was insanely attracted to Henry. Getting to know him as more than just a work partner had definitely been on her list. "I do." She calmly pulled her notebook out of her purse, along with her phone, which also held some information.

Setting her stuff on the table, she gave him a smile. "You ready to break this case wide open?"

Henry chuckled. "You have that much information? Why haven't you said anything?"

Bella shrugged. "Not necessarily. But I figure between the two of us, we can handle this."

He nodded and toyed with his water glass.

Frowning slightly that he didn't seem to be taking this seriously, Bella shook off her reservations and plowed forward. "Okay...first of all, Enoch said someone has been messing with his tools."

Henry nodded again. "I spoke to him and Hope yesterday."

"Great." Bella leaned forward. "But the weird thing is, they didn't take anything."

Henry took a sip of water. "I agree that's odd. Why move them, but not use them?"

"Do you think they're looking for something specific? A certain tool to help them in their job? Or what about our cousin, who's trying to sue us for the inn? Grandma Claire keeps telling me not to worry about it, that her lawyer has it all settled, but there's got to be something there, right? Maybe he stole something?" She paused and frowned. "But why steal? Especially when he's already trying to get the whole thing legally?"

Henry's lips pursed. "Nothing appeared to be out of place in Mrs. Harrison's room."

Bella leaned back. "How do you know?"

"I had a look at it."

"Without me?"

Hank raised an eyebrow. "I didn't know I was supposed to report my every move to you."

Bella folded her arms over her chest. "As partners, I think I definitely should know what you're doing. It's part of the job description." Calling them partners was a bit of a stretch, but Bella was nothing if not determined. If she wanted something, she went after it. She might be full of scraped knees and twisted ankles by the time she got there, but she wasn't one to give up easily.

HANK FELT HIS EYEBROWS rise even higher. "Partners? I thought we were just sharing information?"

Bella clucked her tongue. "Isn't that what partners do?"

Hank closed his eyes for a moment. This is exactly why he hadn't wanted to give into her demands for information. She didn't just want to share what she knew, she wanted to be part of the action. "I am perfectly willing to share everything that happens at the end of the investigation, Bella. You can write your story then."

She slammed her hands on the top of the table, making the water glasses shake slightly. "This isn't just about the story, Henry," she pleaded. For the first time since he'd met her, he heard a bit of vulnerability in her voice. Bella was like a raging storm. She burst into rooms and situations without a care for those around her, leaving a mark wherever she went. And she did it with a stunning smile and innocent-looking face. It was going to get her in trouble some day.

The worst part, however, was the fact that he found himself drawn to the storm. There was something decidedly intriguing about her confidence, her smug grin, her teasing, and even those adorable freckles on her nose. Together they created a package that he wanted to get to know on a much deeper level than being partners in solving a crime.

"Then what is it about?" he asked, trying to act cool. He was trying to hide the fact that he was a softie. Hank had a feeling that if Bella knew he struggled to say no, she would take total advantage of it. He might be a good detective, strong and able to separate himself emotionally from a case, but he'd been raised with four younger sisters. Two of which now had their own daughters. Hank knew all too well that it only took a flutter of their lashes and he was under their thumb.

Bella took a deep breath and closed her eyes for a moment. When she opened them, they were much dimmer than before. "Can I level with you?"

Hank frowned, then leaned forward so their conversation could stay more private. "Of course."

"I know we don't really know each other, Henry, so I'm trusting the fact that you keep secrets for a living."

Hank nodded for her to continue. *What in the world is she so worried about? Is she hiding the fact that she's the thief?* The thought gave him a start. There was no way Bella could be the thief. Was there? She did seem to like attention, but would she go that far?

"I need this," Bella whispered. "Things haven't been going well since graduation. Nobody is interested in the stories I really want to write. I've been showing up at police stations all around my home and no one is willing to even talk to me, let alone let me write anything." She scrunched up her nose. "I've been writing stupid fluff pieces just to get by. But it's not what I want to do."

"What do you want to do?" Relief flooded his system as he realized this wasn't a confession of guilt. Nothing would nip his attraction in the bud like her being a criminal.

"I already told you. I want to be a crime reporter. I want to get in on the nitty-gritty. Investigate behind the scenes, see what makes the mind of the serial killer tick and how the victims overcame their experiences." She took a deep breath. "I want to write stories that intrigue, horrify, and change people."

Hank slowly shook his head. "I don't know that I've ever seen someone get so passionate about the dark, seedy side of life." He frowned. "If that's what you want to do, why the heck are you in Seagull Cove? This missing ring is as exciting as it gets around here."

Bella played with the condensation on her water glass. "Grandma needed help and I was available." She sighed and pushed the glass away. "I'm sure you already knew that though."

Hank nodded, confirming that Sheriff Davidson had said something similar.

"Plus, I needed a change of scenery. I wasn't getting anywhere. Nobody is willing to let me break into the industry, and so I hoped that this might be a little vacation to help reset my confidence." She gave him a crooked grin.

Hank laughed softly. "And then a mystery just fell right into your lap."

"Right?!" Bella exclaimed, her voice sounding much more excited than it had a moment before. "I mean...it seems like such a gift." She leaned forward. "And add in the fact that a hunky detective is the one working the case, and what woman can resist that?"

Hank huffed and grinned. "You don't mince words, do you?" He had to admit to himself that he was flattered though. She hadn't exactly made him think he was hideous, but hearing her say it out loud was good for his ego, and helped in his decision to keep getting to know her.

Bella shrugged. "Why bother? Neither of us will be here for that long, so why not jump right into the thick of it?"

"The seafood scampi?"

Hank turned to the waiter and they waited for the food to be set down. The table was quiet for a few minutes as they both began to eat.

"So...you didn't really answer before," Bella ventured. "Now that I've hung myself out to dry, I'd like to know your thoughts."

Hank paused, wiped his mouth with his napkin, and set it back in his lap. He was purposefully taking a little extra time, his mind spinning with everything she'd said. Yes, he wanted to get to know her, but he still was hesitant about the partner thing. He felt bad that she'd been struggling with her career and wanted to help her, but a stolen ring in a tiny seaside town wasn't going to be the break she was hoping for. Not to mention that his interest in her meant that he had an automatic desire to protect her. Letting her in on the job would mean letting her in on the danger...or at least possible danger. And that went against every grain in his body. "Since you were upfront, I'll be honest as well."

"Thank you, I appreciate that." Bella tilted her head and looked at him with an open expression.

"I'm...torn." He put up a hand before she could interrupt. "I can appreciate that you want to further your career. No one can blame you for that. Although, I have to wonder why you think a petty theft case in Seagull Cove is going to be useful." He leaned in a little. "And I've never been one to turn down time with a beautiful woman, but I am one to protect them. You wanting to be in on the action goes against my instincts."

Bella rolled her eyes. "I don't need protecting, Henry. Like you said, this is a petty theft case. But if I can write a story that actually gets published, even if it is in a small town, it gives me something to put in my portfolio. Right now my resume is full of fluffy pieces because it's the only thing I can get in on." She snorted in disgust. "People think women like me should be in heels rather than running shoes, and it's dumb."

Hank knew if they worked together, he would absolutely protect her, despite her protests. But she had a point about her resume. No one would take her seriously if she didn't have any experience. And the fact that this was such a minimal case should hopefully mean there wasn't any real danger. The whole thing was probably a senile guest, or someone who was hard up on cash. Letting out a long breath, he nodded firmly, his mind made up. "Okay. You can stick around if you want. But!" He held up a finger. "If something starts to go wrong, I want your word that you'll follow what I say. If I tell you to abandon ship, you do it without question. Deal?"

Bella's smile could have lit up every home in their tiny town, and Hank felt himself grow warm at the fact that it was directed at him. "Absolutely." She held her hand over the table, gave him a firm shake, then picked up her fork and began eating again.

Laughing to himself, Hank also went back to his meal. He was starving, though he was trying not to show it. The office had been busy today, hence his wrinkled wardrobe, and he hadn't managed to eat lunch. Having a dinner date with Bella gave him a good excuse to fill up on a heavy meal.

"So...what all will our time together entail?" She quirked an eyebrow at him. "Stakeouts? Filing reports?" She paused. "Kissing?"

Hank choked on the bite of steak in his mouth and had to grab his water to flush it down. When he could finally breathe, he looked over to see her laughing at his reaction.

"I'll take that as a yes," she quipped.

Heaven help me...

CHAPTER 4

Bella found herself restless the next day. Her dinner with Henry had gone quite well, but she was itching to get moving with the mystery. Instead, she was stuck behind the front desk, doodling on her phone's note app.

When the doorbell rang, she rushed to answer as if it was the most exciting thing to happen to her in ages. She laughed at herself before pulling it open. "You're so dumb," she murmured to herself.

Pulling on the door knob, she gave her standard greeting. "Hello! Welcome to the..." She trailed off and put her hand on her hip, cocking it out just a little for a better effect. "Howdy, stranger."

Henry smirked at her. "It's going to be difficult to be a good journalist if you can't remember people you already met only a few hours ago."

Bella put her fingers on her lips. "We've met before? How silly of me." She backed up. "Come on in and I'll search my brain for your name."

Henry tsked his tongue, but wiped his feet and finished coming inside. "I think I'm offended. I even gave you permission to call me by my nickname."

Bella tapped her lip. "Hmm...that does sound familiar. But I have to admit that I wasn't impressed with the nickname." She frowned. "If it's the one I'm thinking of anyway."

Henry raised an eyebrow and stepped up close to her, invading Bella's bubble. Her nerve endings stood on end and she allowed herself to enjoy the shocks running through her body. With her extrovert tendencies, Bella had met quite a few men in her life. Very few had caught her attention, and even fewer had caused a bodily reaction like she was experiencing right now. In fact, she had to give Henry credit. Not one of them had ever affected her quite so strongly as him. She wasn't sure if it was because she was older now and Henry was much more man than her college boyfriends had ever been, or if it was because Henry was...Henry.

"You don't like my name?" he asked, his voice low with just a hint of steel in it.

Bella raised her eyebrows and slowly shook her head. "I didn't say that. I said I didn't like your nickname." She winked. "I'd expect a detective like yourself to catch the difference."

Henry's lips twitched. "That's a new one for me. Most people think my name is old-fashioned."

Bella shrugged daintily and sashayed away from him. "There's nothing wrong with an old, classic-style name. Sure beats being called the same thing as a cowdog." She kept her grin to herself as he chuckled. Their banter was changing her whole day. She wasn't bored anymore. Everything about this situation had her feeling alive and on fire.

"A cowdog, huh?" Henry nodded with his lips pursed. "I've been told I'm like a bloodhound, but never a cowdog."

"Really?" Bella walked around the desk and put her elbow on it, then her chin in her hands, hoping she looked cute and enticing, not like an idiot. "I've been told the same thing."

Henry finished walking her way and leaned across the counter top. "Guess that's just another thing we have in common."

Bella swallowed hard, her mouth going dry at his nearness. The musky scent of his cologne swirled through the air, and she found herself suddenly intimidated by his raw power. This man exuded barely leashed power. He was used to being in charge and getting his way. Bella found herself feeling not quite up to the task of weaseling her way into his investigation.

He might have agreed to let her help last night, but it had been all too obvious he wasn't very keen on the idea. She needed him to want her around, and right now her usually busy brain was completely blank.

"I guess so," she squeaked. Blinking rapidly, she pulled back from their staring contest and forced herself to step back from his magnetic pull. Bella cleared her throat, hoping he hadn't caught the anxious edge in her tone. "So...what brings you by today?"

The curve to Henry's lips let her know that she wasn't fooling anyone and Bella folded her arms over her chest. She knew the stance was defensive, but at the moment, it helped her feel slightly more in control. She rarely found herself at a loss for words and was almost always the one in charge of a situation, so this reversal was a new thing for her, and she wasn't sure she liked it.

"I thought maybe I should do a bit of investigating," he said easily. "I haven't looked around the inn very much. Since I was brought in slightly late to the investigation, I didn't worry about it the other day. Sometimes introductions are enough for one day."

Bella nodded her agreement. "If you'll give me five minutes, I'll be able to go with you." She watched a frown pull at his forehead before he smoothed it out.

"That sounds fine," he replied, straightening from his stance on the desk.

Bella grit her teeth. *So much for falling under his good-looking spell. He really is trying to cut me out of things. Well...too bad! He told me I could be there, and I intend to keep him to his promise.* "If you'd like to take a seat on the bench, I'll get things figured out here."

Henry nodded and walked over to the area she had indicated.

Bella watched his foot bounce as he sat. It was evident he was not used to sitting still. After revealing his true feelings about her coming along, Bella was tempted to make him wait longer, just to see what he'd do about it.

She set the phone up to forward any calls to her cell phone, rather than the front desk, and stuffed her cell in her pocket. "Okay. I'm ready," she said, bouncing out from behind the desk.

She probably should have teased him a little more, maybe put him in his place and let him know who was boss, but the problem was, she was just as eager to get going as he was.

Torturing him would only torture me as well, she thought glumly as she led him up the stairs to Mrs. Harrison's room. Once there, Bella knocked firmly. "Mrs. Harrison? I'm here with Detective Gordon to look at the crime scene."

She turned and glared over her shoulder at his stifled snicker.

"Sorry," he said with a shrug, looking younger and much more approachable than he had when he was flirting with her at the front desk. "I've just never heard someone say it quite like that."

"Well, what would you call it?" she asked in exasperation. This man was starting to drive her nuts. She was attracted to him to the point of distraction, yet he seemed to always have the upper hand when they were together, and now he was making fun of her. How much could a woman take before she punched a guy in the face?

"Usually I just say I'm here to look around."

Bella rolled her eyes. "That's boring." She turned back to the door, which hadn't budged. "Mrs. Harrison?" She knocked again. When no one answered, Bella pulled out her master key. "Guess it won't matter now," she said snippily. "Mrs. Harrison isn't here to appreciate my honesty."

THIS TIME HANK KEPT his chuckle to himself. He'd already put the feisty woman on the defensive, and if he wasn't careful, he would grow to regret it. Kind of like he was regretting saying she could come with him on his investigation.

He really would work much better without her distracting him. Her smell, the sound of her voice, and her quick quips were all enough to drive him crazy, but in a good way.

Few women kept up with him the way she did, and he had to give her credit for doing so. His dry humor and sometimes hard personality usually drove women away. They didn't like to stick around and try to get the best of him. He frowned. The thought made him wonder how long Bella would stick around.

She'd been bold last night, teasing him about kissing and stuff, but that didn't mean she actually wanted anything more than a working relationship with him. He'd recognized she was trying to throw him off his game, and darned if it hadn't worked, though he tried to hide it.

He snorted. *Choking on your steak was not the best way to hide it.*

"What?"

Hank looked up from the dresser he was studying. "What, what?"

Bella stuck out her bottom lip and tapped her foot. "You snorted? Am I doing something wrong?" She looked at the bookshelf she was going through as if it had tattled on her. "I know you said you already looked in here, but am I missing something obvious?"

A smile grew on Hank's face and he shook his head. *Dang, she's cute.* "No. I was just thinking."

"About what?"

He felt the blood rush from his head. There was no way he was telling her he was thinking about the fact that he hoped she was serious about wanting to kiss him. "Nothing," he choked out.

"It can't be nothing."

"Oh, it can."

Bella rolled her eyes. "Why do men always do that? How can you honestly be thinking about nothing?" She shook her head. "It's just not real. Minds are always going."

"Women's maybe," Hank hedged, grateful the subject was shifting. "We men can absolutely be completely blank."

She made a face. "That sounds horrible."

He shrugged. "It's relaxing."

"Whatever." Bella turned back to the bookcase.

Hank studied her. "So...what are you looking for?"

Bella glanced over her shoulder. "I don't know. Something out of the ordinary."

He couldn't help but smile again. Usually he found newbies like her annoying, but she was just so eager...and so off the mark. "While it's good to look over the whole room, the most important part of the room is going to be the place where the valuable was kept."

Bella marched over to him. "So no bookcase?"

"We can look there if you want, but the odds of finding something there? Pretty slim."

She sighed and squished her lips to the side. "Fine. Show me what you're doing."

Hank stepped back and opened up the dresser to her. "Come up here and tell me what you see."

She stepped up close, her shoulder brushing his chest, sending a thrill through him, and Hank caught his breath. This tiny woman packed a powerful punch, but Hank wasn't one to go down easy...he hoped.

"I see a jewelry box," she stated, looking up at him.

Hank nodded encouragingly.

Bella bit her bottom lip and went back to looking at the display.

Hank forced his lungs to move just a little. The way she bit her lip made it look red and plump, and he found himself fighting the idea of kissing it. She was far too enticing for her own good. Suddenly, he realized she was looking at him with a concerned expression on her face. *Crap. Did she catch me watching her mouth?* "What was that?" he croaked out, clearing his throat. He took a long breath, only to breathe in her citrusy perfume, and his heart began to pound. *I'm having a heart attack. At thirty-two years old, a tiny bite-sized woman is gonna put me in the grave.*

"Henry?" Bella reached out and put a hand on his arm. "Are you okay? You look really pale."

Hank coughed and stepped back. "Yeah. Fine." He stepped away from her, his hands on his hips as he sucked in several long breaths, coughing in-between. "Fine," he finally managed in a much more controlled tone. So help him, he was going to conquer this attraction. He couldn't do this while on a job. He was here to fulfill a debt owed to Bill, not to hit on the innkeeper's granddaughter, no matter how enticing she was. "Tell me again what you see. I was lost in thought."

"Lost in something, that's for sure," Bella muttered under her breath, though Hank caught every word.

Hank barked a laugh. "Come on, Belle. Tell me."

She shot him a look and Hank realized he'd given her a nickname. He shrugged, feigning nonchalance. "What? It fits you."

Her look softened and she finally turned away from him, but not before her eyes darted to his lips and back.

Hank cursed in his head. This woman really was trying to kill him.

"Okay...I already said the jewelry box. But I also see a perfume bottle." Bella picked it up and smelled it, then coughed. "Yep. That's what she wears," she wheezed. "You can usually smell her perfume cloud from ten feet away."

Hank chuckled. "A lot of older women are like that. They get to where they can't smell the scent as well, so they put on more until they can smell it."

"Remind me never to get old," Bella grumbled.

"I hate to say it, but it happens to us all," Hank retorted.

Bella sighed, then shrugged. "I suppose there are worse things in life."

"Too true," Hank muttered, forcing his eyes to the dresser top. "Like not making it to old age." He hadn't meant to be quite so gruesome, but in his line of work, that's exactly what he saw sometimes. And truth be told, if Bella really wanted to be a crime reporter, it's what she was going to see as well.

She went still and Hank worried he'd gone too far. "I suppose you're right," she whispered before straightening her shoulders and throwing her hair over her shoulder. "But I digress. Tell me what I'm missing here."

Hank took the change of subject gratefully. His untamed attraction had calmed down at their chosen topic, but it definitely wasn't something he wished to discuss with someone like Bella. She seemed too beautiful and innocent for those discussions. "Right," he said, taking a deep breath. "If you pay attention to the way Mrs. Harrison lays out her things, you'll learn a lot about the woman."

Stepping up as close as he dared, but not close enough that he couldn't keep himself from reaching for her for a sweet kiss, Hank began to go over all the human psychology he'd learned over the years, teaching Bella everything he knew.

I take it back, he thought as she soaked up his information. *This might be more fun than I thought.*

CHAPTER 5

Emory made peppermint bark. Want some?

Bella bit her lip as she waited for an answer. She and Henry had exchanged phone numbers when they'd gone on their first date. Or sort of date. Although he had admitted she was beautiful, he hadn't pressed for anything else between them, despite her not-so-subtle hints.

"I thought detectives were supposed to be renegades. They're supposed to break the rules and go against the flow of traffic," Bella muttered to herself as she looked through the calendar at the front desk. "Hasn't he ever heard of Columbo?"

Once again, Bella was bored. They had an almost full house at the moment, but her job had been very quiet. Ten guest rooms, nine of them full, no children, a few singles, and some older couples. Bella sighed. "I don't know why I allowed Grandma to talk me into this job."

Her phone buzzed against the counter top and she eagerly picked it up.

I've never been into eating trees, especially before lunch.

Bella snickered. "Okay...maybe he's not boring." She punched back a response.

This is a special tree. It's made from European chocolate and this homemade white chocolate stuff she makes with real mint. It's to die for.

To die for? I can't let any crimes be committed on my watch. I can be there in thirty minutes.

Bella did a little dance of victory. She was sure that if she pushed just a little bit more, she not only would get a good story while she was here at Gingerbread Inn, but she'd also get a few memories to take home with her. Ones that just might involve mistletoe and Hallmark movies.

She couldn't help but tap her foot impatiently as she waited for the next thirty minutes to pass. It seemed as if the old grandfather clock was purposefully moving slow just to taunt her. "Come on, come on, come on," she muttered. "Ha!" The minute hand finally landed on the correct time, exactly thirty minutes after Henry said he'd be there.

Bella's eyes automatically went to the door and she stared at it hard, waiting for the doorbell to ring. Another minute passed. "Shoot. He was on time the other night. Why not today?" Bella groaned, letting her head fall to the desk. She ignored the hypocrisy in that statement, knowing she was rarely on time to anything, including her own birthday celebration once.

Just as she hit the wood, the doorbell rang and she sprang upright. Rushing across the foyer, she took a moment to pause and straighten her clothes and hair, then carefully opened the door. "Well, Henry. Fancy meeting you here." Bella put her hand on her hip and hoped it looked seductive. Her tiny frame didn't always pull that look off very well. She usually looked like a child trying to be an adult.

His dark eyes sparkled with humor, then changed to concern. "Are you hurt?" Henry stepped up to her and touched her forehead. "What happened?"

Bella leaned back from his warm touch, and fingered her forehead. *Oh my gosh. I'm such an idiot.* She had apparently drowned in her sorrows a little too much, causing a bump on her forehead from hitting the desk. "It's nothing," she hurried to say. Backing up, she ushered him in. "Let's close the door before Mother Nature thinks she's invited in as well."

"We wouldn't want that," Henry said, stepping fully inside and starting to take off his coat. "Especially with tree bark waiting for me. She might get jealous."

Bella snorted and took his coat, walking it to the front closet. "You're hilarious. A regular comedian."

Henry was smirking at her as she came back. "Think I should quit my day job?"

Bella sidled up to him and looked up. "Probably not. I mean, with that much talent, you're just going to make the rest of us look bad."

Henry laughed and held out his elbow. "Can I escort you to this treat you promised me?"

"Hang on." Bella rushed to the front desk, grabbed the cordless receiver, and tucked it in her back pocket. "Okay. Now you may."

She slipped her hand into his elbow and reveled in the feel of his muscles beneath the shirt. She could feel them flex as they walked, and it was far more enticing than the chocolate they were headed for. "In there." Bella pointed to the kitchen door.

Henry held it open for her and Bella strutted ahead, as if she owned the room.

"Hey, Bel, whatcha need?" Emory asked after glancing quickly over her shoulder. She paused, however, when Henry followed Bella in. "Detective Gordon." Emory turned, grabbing a towel from her shoulder and wiping her hands on it. "Is there something I can help you with?"

"I'm afraid I was lured here by the promise of chocolate," Henry said a little sheepishly. He scratched at his jawline and looked to Bella for help.

She almost stood back and let him suffer a little, but she still hadn't gotten a kiss from the handsome man, so she decided not to push her luck. "I invited him to come try your peppermint bark," Bella explained.

"Gotcha." Emory nodded firmly, all business as usual. "Let me just plate some up."

"Don't go to any trouble," Henry said quickly.

"I can just grab the jar," Bella piped up, knowing it would drive Emory crazy.

True to her reputation, Emory stopped and glared at her cousin. "There will be no grabbing," she stated fiercely. "If you'll take your guest to the dining room, I'll bring some in for the two of you."

Bella tried to bite back her smile, but she couldn't help it. Emory was far too predictable. "Anything you say, dear cousin," Bella said sweetly. She caught Emory rolling her eyes and the laughter Bella had been holding back bubbled up and out.

Grabbing Henry's hand, she led him into the dining room and planted him in a chair.

"I didn't realize it was going to be such a big deal," he said, his cheeks slightly pink under a few day's beard growth.

Bella sat down beside him and crossed her legs, angling her calf his way. *A girl has to use every advantage she can,* she reminded herself. "Nah...it's not a big deal. Emory's always been like that."

He raised a single eyebrow at her. "Why do I get the feeling that you take shameless advantage of that fact?"

Bella laughed and threw her hair over her shoulder. "Because you're an amazing detective," she teased back, then leaned in. "Obviously, nothing gets past you."

HANK SWALLOWED HARD. Was the room hotter than it should be? He glanced around for a fireplace, making sure to keep his eyes off Bella's lovely legs, sitting oh-so-perfectly for his perusal. She was wearing a modest knee-length skirt and a blouse that was buttoned up to where it should be. But the tiny, fierce package inside those clothes was proving to be quite irresistible to him.

He'd dated a few women in his time, but never had he had one who was so clear about making her interest known. It was heady and a bit intimidating at the same time. Was he supposed to just give in and jump into a relationship? They both had a timeline, and Hank wasn't really into things with an expiration date. Bella was definitely different than the other women he'd known. He was afraid she would get under his skin, and when the mystery was gone and she went back to California for her job, he would find a hole in his life...and possibly his heart.

"Your flattery isn't going to work on me," Hank said, pushing his attraction to the back burner. He was an adult, he could handle this. Even if his inner voice was demanding he find some mistletoe ASAP.

"Really?" She drew the word out. "Whyever not?"

Hank leaned in close, trying not to let the spicy smell of her go to his head. "Because I'm too old for those tricks. I'm a detective, remember? I've seen every trick in the book."

"I definitely didn't forget you were a detective," she responded, not budging an inch at his nearness. "I'm just hoping you don't forget that you're a man and I'm a woman."

"I don't think forgetting that is possible," he replied without thinking. His words sent a charge through the air and the moment felt thick and sticky. Her eyes grew wide for a split second, then that playful smirk tugged at her lips. The inviting look immediately drew his gaze and he couldn't seem to pull his gaze away from her. Slowly, hesitatingly, he leaned in. A small part of him knew it was too soon, but the other part didn't care. This fierce woman in front of him was capturing his attention, and he was quickly growing tired of trying to stay aloof.

"Here we go," Emory said, bustling into the room. She skidded to a halt. "Um...sorry." Emory shrank back a little as Hank straightened and cleared his throat.

"No...I'm sorry," he said, turning to Emory. "I got a little carried away."

"Not carried away enough," Bella muttered.

Emory must have been used to her cousin's comments because she simply made a face and moved forward again. "I'll, uh, just drop this off and get out of your way." She kept her eyes down, a sure sign she was still embarrassed over what she had almost interrupted, and Hank didn't know what to say to make it better.

He was embarrassed as well. Embarrassed he'd given into wanting to kiss her this quickly after knowing her, as if he was some undisciplined teenage boy, driven by his hormones instead of his brain. He was also embarrassed that someone had seen him being unprofessional when he'd been hired to do a job.

"Thank you," he said softly as Emory set a beautiful tray on the table. "It looks delicious."

She smiled at him, only holding his eyes for a second. "Thanks. It's really a pretty easy dessert, but people love it, so I try to make it every year."

"I've never had it, so I'm excited to try it." He looked down and realized she'd brought much more than a plate of chocolate pieces. There was the promised peppermint bark, plus two cups of hot cocoa, which had a small hint of cinnamon if the smell was anything to go by, a couple of biscuit-looking things, and two glasses of milk. "Whoa..."

"Thanks, Em!" Bella called out as her cousin disappeared. She smiled widely at Hank. "Emory lives for food. She can't help but try to nurture everyone around her with it. No matter what ails you, she has something that will fix it."

"I can see that." Everything on the try was set just right and it showed exactly what type of personality Emory was. Driven, no-nonsense, and detail oriented. It probably served her well in her chosen profession. "I never thought I'd say this, but it's almost too pretty to eat." He slowly picked up one of the long biscuit things. "My small-town upbringing is probably showing, but what exactly is this?"

Bella laughed, a sound of joy, not teasing, and Hank couldn't help but smile with her. "That's biscotti. It's one of her specialties and totally worth all the calories it has." She picked up her own piece. "You have to try it in the hot chocolate. It's kind of hard on it's own, but soaked in chocolate? Mmm..." Bella gushed. "It's amazing."

"I'll take your word for it," he mumbled, daring to dip it as she suggested. A sandy, vanilla flavor slid across his tongue and he groaned. "Wow. Your cousin is an artist."

Bella's bright smile slipped for just a second before she plastered it back on. "She is. I always have to watch my figure when I'm around her." Hank didn't miss the way she subtly turned her body away from him, going from openly inviting to slightly closed off.

It didn't take a genius to figure out what was going on. Knowing he had to nip this in the bud before it went any further, Hank reached out and took her chin, bringing Bella's beautiful face back to his. "Thank you for the invitation," he said in a low voice. "I wouldn't have stepped away from work for just anybody."

The pink in her cheeks let him know his words were doing their job. Slowly, he let his fingers slide along her jaw and chin, enjoying the smooth feel of her skin. He let his fingers slide to her cheek and then tuck her hair behind her ear. His hand then slid through her hair, coming down to the end and letting the silkiness slip through his fingers.

"Are you saying I should feel special?" she asked, her voice slightly breathless.

Hank grinned. "You should."

"I have a confession to make."

He raised his eyebrows in invitation.

"Flattery absolutely works on me."

Hank chuckled and leaned in closer, the moment they had lost rushing back all at once. "Good to know," he murmured just as their lips brushed. Heat rushed through him from that simple touch and he almost pulled back. It was just as he'd suspected. Starting something with this woman was going to be different than any other relationship he'd ever had, which meant their possible parting when they both went back to their lives was going to be different as well.

Bella didn't seem to have any of his reservations, however, as she leaned in and brought their mouths fully together, slamming him with more sensations than he'd thought one body could hold. When she grabbed the front of his shirt, he groaned and wrapped his arms around her, pulling her into his lap with a quick jerk.

A thud overhead went unnoticed as he got lost in the feel of the petite woman in his arms. She felt so perfectly right. He'd never believed in soulmates, but this was a whole other level of connection that he hadn't known existed.

Another loud thud sounded above them, and this time his ear tuned in to the sound. When it was followed by a scream and some shouting, Hank forced himself to pull back. Both he and Bella were breathing heavily, but he forced himself to think on what was happening upstairs. "Did you hear that?"

A loud crash sounded and more screaming ensued.

"What in the world?" Bella looked up with her jaw open.

"Stay here," Hank ordered, gently lifting her off his lap as quickly as he could and darting to the doorway.

"Over my dead body!" Bella called out, running after him.

Hank cursed in his mind, knowing her refusal to listen was just a sign of things to come, but he ran on anyway. Something important was going on upstairs and he needed to be there.

CHAPTER 6

Taking a second to ditch her high heels, Bella raced out of the dining room from a closer door to the stairs. She grinned. Henry didn't know this house as well as she did.

"Bella!" he yelled from where he was now behind her.

Ignoring his call, she dashed up the stairs as quickly as she could in her pencil skirt. It hindered her leg movements more than she wanted it to, but right now was *not* the time to worry about it. Henry wasn't far behind her, and if her ears were to be believed, Bella could tell he was gaining ground.

The crashing sounds had stopped, but screams of anger and distress were still ringing through the house. A couple of doors opened as she rushed down the hall, but Bella didn't stop. She could hear Henry asking everyone to stay in their rooms.

She slid to a stop, nearly toppling head over heels on the shiny hardwood boards.

"It was supposed to be me," someone said, tears evident in the sound.

Bella grabbed the handle, trying desperately to catch her breath. "What in this world?" she asked with wide eyes as she opened the door. It looked like a hurricane had swept through. Shards of porcelain and glass were scattered all over the carpet. Hope lay sprawled on her backside, one hand on a bleeding cheek, while Enoch was crouched over a woman. The woman was struggling and screaming against his tight hold.

"Bella, can you call the police, please?" Enoch said, his voice strained.

"I'm here," Henry said from behind Bella. He pulled a pair of handcuffs out of his back pocket and walked up to Enoch. "Just bring her hands in front here."

Bella watched, wide-eyed and fascinated, as Henry cuffed the woman and led her away from the scene, hissing and spitting like a wild cat. Several more people were working their way down the hall, and Henry had to navigate between them to get the woman downstairs and outside.

She made a mental note to follow him to the police station in a few minutes. But first, Bella wanted to make sure Hope was okay. Her cheek was bleeding freely and she appeared to be in shock.

Enoch was holding her, but neither appeared to be in a hurry to move. Walking carefully over the broken decorations, Bella squatted down to their level. "Enoch?" she asked softly, afraid of startling the couple.

He looked at her, his eyes seeming lost and afraid.

""I'm sorry to break this up, but I think Hope needs medical attention on that cheek," Bella said, keeping her tone calm.

"And the rest of us need an explanation," Grandma Claire called from the entrance to the room. She sighed loudly. "And I'll need to speak to the Mendelsons about the damage to their property."

"I think that's the least of our worries," Bella muttered.

"Says the girl who doesn't have to keep this inn running for the next twenty years," Grandma snapped. Bella ducked her head, knowing her comment had been in bad taste.

As Grandma and Enoch spoke to each other, Bella watched Emory and Antony show up at the door as well. She almost asked why Antony was at the house, but decided against it. *One thing at a time,* she reminded herself.

"An ambulance is on the way," Emory said, her eyes darting everywhere. She was obviously uncomfortable with the situation.

Or embarrassed to be caught with Antony. Bella shook her head. "Enough," she scolded herself. Instead of speaking up, Bella followed Enoch and Hope down to the grand foyer, where they sat down to wait.

Only minutes later, a knock on the door came and Bella practically leapt across the space. "I got it. You two just sit tight." She pulled the large door open wide. "Thanks for coming so quickly," Bella said. "Hope is hurt. She's over there." Bella waved them in the right direction.

The paramedics quickly went to work and Bella stood back to watch. Eventually Hope and Enoch left for the hospital so Hope could get some stitches.

Now that her cousin was in good hands, Bella grew restless. Henry would be interrogating the woman, and Bella was being left out!

Hurrying to the sitting room, Bella found her grandmother next to the fire, warming her legs and reading a book. "Grams, I'm heading to the police station."

Grandma Claire peered over her reading glasses. "Whyever are you going there?"

Bella gave her an exasperated look. "Because I want to be there when they talk to that woman."

"*That woman* is Trisha Bingham. She was my housekeeper before I had to shut down." Grandma's face was stern.

"Oooh...that explains a lot," Bella said, tapping her bottom lip, her mind going crazy with ideas. "Do you think she needed the money?"

Grandma shook her head. "From the way she attacked Hope, I think it had more to do with Enoch."

"Duh!" Bella bounced the palm of her hand off her forehead. "Love. It's always the problem, isn't it?"

"Love is a problem?" Grandma began to grumble. "It's no wonder none of you girls are married yet. Love isn't a problem, it's the only thing worth living for."

Bella laughed, thinking of her grandmother and the sheriff, who obviously liked each other, but hadn't done anything about it for years. She crossed the large room to give her grandmother a kiss on the cheek. "Give us time," she teased. "We're still young. We've got plenty of time before we need to get saddled with a family."

"By your age, I'd been married for years and had two children," Grandma continued. "You girls are far more worried about your careers nowadays than you are about families."

Bella shook her head. She had plenty of years left before she needed a family. First, she wanted to see the world and write about it. She wanted to win awards and have fun. And right now, she also wanted to watch the man who had given her a foundation-shaking kiss interrogate a criminal. "Be back soon!"

Ignoring Grandma's grumblings, she grabbed her keys and headed out. The front desk could wait. Right now, Bella had a mystery to solve.

HANK HAD NO IDEA HOW he'd gone from the best kiss of his life to dragging a screaming woman into a police station, but in his line of work, he shouldn't really be surprised.

"BILL!" Hank yelled as he got inside. The woman at the front desk stared at him with wide eyes. "Get Sheriff Davidson, please," Hank asked as kindly as possible as his suspect tried to kick him in the shin again. "You might as well just calm down, miss. You're not going anywhere."

"He was supposed to fall in love with me!" she screeched, then broke down crying. She let her legs go limp and Hank almost lost hold of her as she slumped to the floor.

"What in tarnation is going on here?" Bill growled, storming out from his office. The police station at Seagull Cove wasn't very large, since the town was so small, and soon the entire police force was standing in the waiting room, looking at the spectacle.

"Trisha?" one of the policemen asked, stepping forward. "What are you doing?"

"Go away, Dallin," she whined.

"Trisha Bingham?" Another police officer shook his head.

"You know her?" Hank snapped, still struggling to hold on.

They both shook their heads. "She was a couple years behind me in school," the first officer said sheepishly.

"My daughter was in her grade," the older one explained.

"SHUT UP!" Trisha screamed, climbing back to her feet. "None of you know anything." Her wailing grew to a feverish pitch.

"Bring her back here, son," Bill said, waving Hank down the hallway. "Ms. Rodriguez?"

"Yes, sir?" the secretary responded.

"Get in a call to Dr. Phelps." Sheriff Davidson sighed. "I have a feeling we're going to need her."

"On it, sir."

Hank managed to wrangle Trisha into a room and put her in a chair. Flexing his fingers, he walked around the desk and took a seat himself. He looked at the suspect. Her dark, stringy hair was plastered to her wet face and thick lines of mascara smeared across her skin. Her skinny shoulders shook as she wept, and for a moment, he felt bad for her. Obviously, something had driven her over the deep end to behave this way.

I'm just glad Bella isn't here to witness all this. At that thought, he felt a small pang of sorrow. With the case solved, he'd go back to working in the next town over. Even though it wasn't far, it would make seeing Bella difficult. And after that kiss they shared, he wasn't quite ready to let her go yet.

Sheriff Davidson came in, closing the door behind him. He set a steaming Styrofoam cup on the desk in front of Trisha, then held out his hand to Hank. Letting out a long breath, Hank handed over the keys to the cuffs. If Bill was comfortable letting her go, Hank would trust that, but this woman definitely seemed like a flight risk.

"There now, Miss Trisha," the sheriff said in a gravelly tone. "You just have a drink of this and settle on down."

Trisha glared at him, but took the offering after rubbing her wrists for a moment.

Hank refused to feel bad. If she hadn't fought so hard, the cuffs wouldn't have hurt her.

Bill sat next to Hank with a tired grunt. "Now, Trisha, I've known you your whole life. Suppose you tell me exactly what's going on."

"Don't I get a phone call or lawyer or something?" she demanded.

Hank leaned back and stayed silent. Bill obviously had history with this woman and it would be best to let him work it out.

The sheriff nodded slowly. "You are entitled to a lawyer...if you want one." He tilted his head. "Do you feel you need one, sweetheart? No one here is trying to hurt you. We just want answers."

Trisha's bottom lip trembled and Hank was hard-pressed to stay strong. He hated it when women cried, even if they were criminals. *Or accused criminals. I guess we haven't actually charged her with anything yet.*

She sniffled and wiped her nose on her sleeve. "It doesn't matter," she mumbled forlornly. "It's all over now anyway."

"Tell us about it," Sheriff Davidson encouraged. "And then we'll get you whatever help you need."

Hank was surprised by the grandfatherly way this man was handling the situation. Yes, the town was small and he probably knew just about everyone, but with as many years in the force as Bill had had, Hank would have expected him to be...hardened.

Trisha didn't speak up, so Bill continued.

"Are you the one who's been causing trouble at Gingerbread Inn?" he asked softly.

Trisha froze, then nodded. "Yes. I just..." She looked up with her red-rimmed eyes. "I just wanted Enoch to love me. He did." Her grip on the cup tightened and Hank had a moment's worry she would crush it. "He loved me before Claire's granddaughter showed up. The skank."

The door opened and everyone turned to look at who was intruding.

"I'm his partner, so I'm allowed to be here. Thank you," Bella said sweetly to the officer standing at the door. He looked like he wanted to argue, but when Bella flashed a wide smile, the officer nodded and pulled the door closed behind her.

"Bella." Hank groaned, throwing back his head. "What are you doing?"

Her offended look was almost comical. "I'm here to help you." Tilting her head, she batted her eyelashes. "Exactly like you said I could."

"I never—"

"Isabella," Sheriff Davidson said kindly, but firmly. "This isn't a meeting for you."

Her jaw clenched and Hank recognized the stubborn glint in her eyes. Folding her arms over her chest, Bella began to tap her foot. "I have every right to be here. Henry told me we would work together, and as a journalist, I'm covering the situation. You can't kick me out. The public has a right to know."

"She also has a right to privacy," the sheriff pointed out.

Bella looked at Trisha, who was watching everything with wide eyes. "Trisha...it is Trisha, right?"

Trisha frowned, but nodded.

"Do you mind if I'm here? Don't you think that having a woman around will be helpful? Nobody will understand your concerns more than another woman, right?"

Trisha watched her for several long seconds and Hank held his breath. If Bella got her way, there'd be no end to her crowing. Finally, Trisha nodded. "I think that might be nice." She pointed a finger at Bella. "But I don't want you making me out to be the bad guy. I've been wronged."

Bella nodded, but her face wasn't quite convinced. "Nothing but the bare facts. Got it." She grabbed a chair out of the corner and sat down at the side of the desk, halfway between the men and Trisha. "I'll just listen and help out when needed."

Hank closed his eyes and prayed for strength. This woman seemed bent on upsetting his life.

CHAPTER 7

Bella sat, completely unsatisfied, as an officer led Trisha away. As soon as the door closed, she spun to look at Henry and Sheriff Davidson. "What are we going to do now? None of this is solved yet."

Henry leaned back in his seat, his arms folded over his chest and looking cool as a cucumber. "We solved the missing ring. I'd say that's something."

Bella rolled her eyes. "Yes. But what about the food? The moving tools? The garden supplies out in the yard? The open doors," she said in exasperation, naming all the weird things that had been happening. "Trisha says she didn't do any of that."

Henry stood from his seat and walked over to her seat, holding out a hand. "Come on, Sleuth, our work for now is done."

"But we haven't done anything!" Bella cried, taking his hand and jumping to her feet.

"We've figured out what we can," Sheriff Davidson said from his place still at the table. He was taking notes on a pile of paperwork. "Trisha will see a doctor and we'll take it from there. Meanwhile, no more jewelry should go missing."

Bella sighed and allowed Henry to lead her from the police station. They had been inside so long that it was now dark out and the already cool temperature had plummeted even more. Bella shivered and rubbed her hands up and down her arms.

"Where did you park?" Henry asked.

She shook her head. "I can't go home yet. We need to figure this out."

Henry sighed and turned her to face him. Cupping her face, he gave her a soft, too short kiss. "Bella, we caught a criminal tonight. Take the victory and be grateful."

"But-" He kissed her again, stopping her complaint. "Henry-" He kissed her again. Frustrated, Bella put her hands against his chest. "Quit distracting me!"

Henry smirked and leaned back. "But it worked."

She glared. "That's not the point. The point is we still have another problem."

Henry nodded thoughtfully. "Yes, we do. Like, when do I get to take you to dinner again?"

She groaned and threw her forehead against his chest. "You're impossible."

"Thank you."

Bella laughed, shaking against him. "That sounds like something I would say." She leaned her head back to look into his dark eyes. His gentle fingers brushed a chunk of hair off her forehead.

"Maybe that's why the world shifted when we kissed earlier, huh?"

Her eyebrows shot up. "Wow. And you called me bold."

Henry shrugged. "I suppose neither of us are ones to beat around the bush."

Belle relaxed and laid her cheek against his chest. "Are you going home now? After all, you were hired to find the ring, which is done."

His chest deflated a little, as he let out a long breath. "I suppose I can find a reason to stick around a bit longer."

Bella grinned. "And why is that?"

"Because a woman I'm interested in is going to go poking her nose into other people's business again. So I need to be here to make sure she doesn't do anything reckless."

"Hey!"

Henry chuckled and kissed the top of her head. "Come on. Let's get you home and we'll talk tomorrow. It's late."

Bella sighed, not quite ready to leave the protection of his warm body, but knowing he was right. Besides, she had a lot of planning to do. Something was still wrong at the inn, and she was determined to set it to rights. *Especially since Trisha doesn't want me to really say what happened. How do I write this but NOT make her the bad guy?* Bella made a face. She'd been hesitant to agree, but her curiosity had won out. Bella decided it was at least a lesson to be learned. The more she knew about criminals and their stories, the more she would understand when the opportunity did come to write about it.

"Umm...Bella?"

She turned back to him. "What?'

Henry made a sheepish face. "Can you give me a ride to the inn? A police car brought me here."

She smiled and swung her keys on her finger. "The big bad detective needs some help, huh?"

Henry rolled his eyes and gave her a dry look. "Is that how we're playing this?"

"You better believe it."

Taking a couple steps forward, he broke into her personal space and brought them nose to nose. "Bella...beautiful, courageous writer of crime reporting. Would you please condescend to help out a humble public servant in need of a ride?"

She tried to hold back, she really did, but what girl could keep a straight face with that kind of line? Laughing, Bella stepped back so she didn't whack him in the face as her body shook. "That was terrible." She sighed and wiped at her eye. "I know I told you flattery works, but it at least has to be good flattery. That was like a poem by a second-grader."

Without warning, he grabbed her and gave her a hard kiss. "Please?" Henry whispered against her lips before kissing her again.

"Good grief, that I can't argue with," Bella said breathlessly when he finally let her go. She couldn't help but notice the way his chest puffed up and he sauntered to the car door. "Don't let it go to your head," she called after him.

"Too late!"

Snickering, Bella followed and then thanked him when Henry opened her door and let her slip inside. Once he was in the passenger side, she started the car and pulled out onto the street. "So what are the plans for tomorrow?"

"You mean besides you meeting me for dinner?"

Bella didn't even bother to hide her too-wide smile. "Yeah...besides that."

"I'm sure for the most part, I'll be filling out paperwork about Ms. Bingham."

"I sense a but in that."

"But I'll try to come out first thing in the morning to update the household on everything."

Bella sat up straighter. "What exactly does first thing mean?" She could practically feel Henry's stare.

"Are you telling me you're a late riser?"

Bella scrunched up her nose as she took a turn with the car. "I might be a late everything," she admitted.

Henry chuckled. "I'll make sure it's after the inn has opened. Is that all right?"

"That'll work," she said with a dramatic sigh. Yet even as they made the plans, she knew she'd be wide awake in the morning. Between the churning of her mind about the case and the fast beat of her heart because of Henry, Bella knew sleep wouldn't be on her agenda at all.

HANK COULDN'T HELP but laugh a little as he climbed the steps of Gingerbread Inn the next morning. "Is she awake or still sleeping?" was the question of the morning. It hadn't surprised him at all when Bella had said she was a late everything-type person.

She wasn't the type to follow all the rules, whether written or not. Yet, her quirks and eagerness were part of why he was drawn to her. He did tend to be a rule follower, and seeing someone so free and excited about life was alluring.

He rang the doorbell and was surprised when it opened quickly.

"Morning, Sherlock," Bella chirped, letting him inside. She grinned. "Surprised?"

Hank shook his head and leaned down to kiss the top of her head. "Nope. I think the fact that you had to admit to be a late sleeper last night meant that you would automatically be up early this morning. You don't like to be tied down by titles."

She whistled low. "And people say I'm good at reading the situation."

Hank grinned as he shrugged out of his jacket. "It's part of the job description."

"Yeah, well...you and I might be on time, but poor Hope is still sleeping."

Hank paused. "Is that normal for her?"

Bella shook her head. "No. She's like Emory. Early riser."

"That's what I figured. You're the only rebel of the group." He laughed and danced away when Bella tried to punch him in the arm.

"Watch it, buster," she said, pointing a finger at him. "I have control over whether or not you get one of Emory's orange rolls this morning."

A knock came on the door behind him. As Bella passed to open it, he caught her around the waist. "You wouldn't really deny me a treat, would you?" he whispered against her ear.

Bella pulled away and straightened her shirt. "Watch me."

Hank chuckled and shook his head. He loved bantering with Bella. The more they did it, the more he loved it. Conversations with her were lively and exhilarating, keeping him coming back for more.

"Hank," Sheriff Davidson said with a nod. He took his hat off and tossed it onto a nearby bench. "I'm assuming we're both here for the same reason?"

Hank nodded. "I figured the family needed to know what happened yesterday."

"Agreed, son. Agreed." Bill slapped Hank on the shoulder, then headed toward the kitchen. "I smell something delicious," he mumbled, to Hank and Bella's amusement.

"Come on, Detective," Bella said, grabbing his hand. "Let's get in there."

Thirty minutes later, Hope had joined them, and the kitchen was full of chatter as the gathered group went over everything that had happened, including Enoch and Hope's trip into some hidden passageways inside the mansion.

"Crap! I can't believe I forgot!" Enoch cried, hurrying from the kitchen. "Be right back."

The whole room paused as they waited for the handyman to appear again. "What's he doing?" Hank whispered to Bella.

"I don't know," she answered with a shrug.

A minute or two later, Enoch came back holding a dish in his hands.

"My pie!" Emory cried, walking to meet him and grab the porcelain plate. "I knew it! I told you someone took my pie. And they ate it just like they did my nougat."

Hank stepped forward. "Where did you find that?" he asked Enoch.

"When I was walking around in the walls, I ended up in a hidden attic," Enoch explained. "There was a bunch of blankets, an old pair of boots, and a small table." He pointed to the pie plate. "That was on the table."

"So someone's living in the attic?" Bella asked, her voice sounding excited. Hank wanted to groan again. He had hoped the missing food was just coincidence and that he could convince Bella to give up her chase. Apparently that wasn't going to happen.

Hank scribbled some notes in his notebook and stuffed it in his back pocket. "It seems like you're right, Ms. Hope. I think we have more than one person causing trouble around here."

"Oh my gosh, this is exciting," Bella gushed. "And here I thought it would all end with the crazy lady behind bars."

Heaven help us. "I'm going to go check things out," he said to Enoch.

"The entrance is in the laundry room," the handyman explained. "I probably didn't close it properly since I was in a hurry, so it'll be easy to see."

Hank nodded his thanks and headed out.

"The laundry room is this way," Bella said, walking away from him.

Hank hurried to catch up. "I don't suppose I can convince you to stay here?"

She gave him a fierce look and Hank sighed. He seemed to be doing that a lot lately. "There it is." She headed straight for the wall where a small door was slightly ajar.

"Uh, uh, uh," Hank hurried to intercept her. "I realize I can't stop you from coming, but you would please let me go first?"

Bella put her hands on her hips and tapped her foot. "Afraid a girl can't handle it?"

"No. I'm afraid of what will happen if someone jumps out and tries to hurt you."

"Because you don't think I can defend myself?" she scoffed.

"No." Hank shook his head harder and stepped closer. "I'm not afraid for you, Belle. I'm afraid of what I'll do to the other person."

Bella's eyes widened, and for the first time, she looked shocked. Swallowing hard, she dropped her gaze and nodded. "I don't think I can argue with that."

"Thank you." Hank knew he'd been pretty intense, but he was dead serious. Bella was squirming her way right into his heart, and he didn't want her hurt. And with her way of bumbling into any and all situations, he had no doubt she would eventually end up that way. Letting him go first eased his protective instincts and allowed him to do his job with less distraction.

Eyeing the doorway, Hank stepped forward, only pausing to turn on the flashlight feature on his cell phone. It was going to be a tight fit to get himself through the doorway. "People must have been smaller back in the day," he grunted as he stepped through, brushing the doorway on both sides.

As soon as he was inside, he had to brush cobwebs out of his face.

"Ewww..." Bella whined behind him. "This place is nasty."

"I'll be sure and tell the housekeeper," Hank muttered as he began to walk forward.

Bella snickered. "I don't know that we'll get Hope in here again. She seems to have had her fill of adventure."

"I guess you got all those genes?" he asked, his mind only partly on the conversation. He was looking for the stairs that Enoch had said were straight ahead. "Gotcha," he whispered when they came into view.

Putting his free hand on the railing, he slowly began to climb, being careful to watch his weight on each stair.

"Probably," Bella continued. "I can't imagine sitting around quietly on my days off."

"Or just being quiet in general," he teased, laughing softly when she whacked his back.

"I could be worse, you know," Bella shot back.

"Yeah? How's that?"

"I could be as loud as Trisha."

Hank winced. That woman's screaming had been loud enough to wake the dead. "Well, let's hope you don't fall into unrequited love and decide to go on a crime spree. I'm sure that brings out the worst in anybody."

There was a pause in their conversation, with only the groaning of the house keeping them from utter silence. "Is it wrong to feel sorry for her?" Bella finally whispered.

Hank shook his head. "No. In fact, feeling sorry for her is a good sign." He reached back with his free hand and squeezed when she held on. "Never let your job make you hard, Belle. That would be a far worse tragedy."

CHAPTER 8

Things had quieted down considerably since Trisha had been taken into custody, but Bella couldn't seem to find any kind of peace in the situation. And despite the lack of chaos, the situation still wasn't resolved.

Emory was losing food at an alarming rate, but it seemed like most of the men thought it was just a hungry guest who was sneaking in in the middle of the night.

Bella's nose twitched and she tapped her foot angrily. "Something is wrong...I can feel it."

"And your toes are going to fix it?"

Bella spun and scowled. "Who let you in?"

Henry's eyebrows shot up. "I wasn't aware I was so unwelcome."

Bella's shoulders sank. "You are welcome, I just didn't hear you come in." She squished up one side of her face. "I must be going deaf."

Henry chuckled and came closer. "You're not deaf. I came in by a back door."

She instantly picked up. "Why?"

Henry's steps faltered ever so slightly as he finished walking to her side. "I was looking at something."

"What?"

Henry tilted his head. "Something."

She shook her head at him. "Nope. that won't work, Henry. You promised."

Henry sighed and pinched the bridge of his nose. "Can't you let anything go?"

"Nope."

He held out his hand. "Fine. Come with me."

Bella eagerly grabbed hold and let him guide her around to the far side of the house. Once there, he let go of her hand and waited. She frowned, glancing around. A cold wind wrapped around her and she shivered, wrapping her arms around herself. "I'm gonna freeze to death if you don't tell me why you were here soon."

With a snort, he took off his own coat and wrapped it around her.

His familiar scent permeated the fabric and Bella found herself sinking into the warmth.

"I want you to use your newfound skills to figure out why I'd be out here," Henry explained. He stuffed his hands into his front pockets and Bella immediately felt guilty that she had his coat. She started to take it off, but he stopped her. "Don't even think about it," he growled softly. "My mother would flip a switch if she knew I was wearing a coat and not you." He smiled and used the collar to drag her a little closer. "Besides," he said softly, kissing her forehead, "you look very cute, and I'm the one who dragged you outside without protection."

"Only after I told you to," she shot back, but nuzzled into the soft coat. "And thank you."

"You're welcome." He turned her around and put his hands on her shoulders. "Now. Look."

Bella rolled her eyes. "I feel like we're having a Mr. Miyagi moment here, or something. You're always telling me to look, but not telling me what I'm looking for."

"I'm getting cold, Belle, better figure it out before I take us back inside."

Bella held back a swoon at his use of her nickname. She absolutely adored it when he called her that. No one else did and for some reason, that made the act more special, more intimate. Forcing her mind to focus, she put her eyes on the side of the house. They were standing at a door. One that led to the hallway with the laundry room, if Bella was remembering correctly. She glanced to her right, noting that the garden shed was just across the lawn. "This is where the door was left open the other day," she murmured.

"Good," Henry responded. "Keep going."

Holding the coat tightly closed, she stepped closer. "A garden rake was also left out around here, but the shed was locked." She started to walk toward the shed, but Henry made a beeping noise.

"Cold...cold...colder..."

She stopped and turned to look at him incredulously. "Are you playing hot and cold with me? Really? What are we? Five?"

Henry winked at her but said nothing else.

Huffing as dramatically as she could, she turned to the house.

"Warmer..."

Bella shot Hank a look, but his smirk never wavered. Her eyes immediately went to the door, but she couldn't find anything amiss. She crouched down, shivering slightly despite the borrowed coat, and studied the doorknob. "I don't see any scratching or anything." She squinted up at him. "That means no forced entry, right?"

Henry nodded slowly. "A scratched doorknob isn't the only sign, but yes, there are no signs of forced entry."

"So what did you find of interest out here?"

"Keep going," he urged.

Bella pinched her lips together, equal parts frustrated and eager to prove herself. Finally, she dropped her eyes to the ground. The grass was brown and dry, the ground hard with the cold weather, and dark from the moisture in the air. As she looked around the stoop, she noticed something unusual. "Crumbs," she murmured. Bending down, she picked up a few small brown chunks. They were lighter in color than the dirt, more of a caramel or honey tone, and there were several in a clump at the bottom of the steps. "Crumbs!" she called out to Henry, holding them up. "Our food thief was out here!"

Henry smiled at her, pride shining in his eyes. "Very good, Belle."

Bella stood up and brushed off her hands. “But what does it mean? We know they came this way, but they didn’t have to force their way into the mansion. Which still means it could possibly be a guest. I mean...they could have stepped outside to eat, then come right back in.”

Henry grunted in a noncommittal fashion, took her sleeve-covered hand, and led her back inside. Once there, he took his coat back and hung it on the rack. “Do you mind if we warm up by the fire?”

Bella shook her head. “No. That’s fine. Would you like some hot chocolate or apple cider?”

“Like I’d ever turn that down,” Henry responded with an easy grin.

“Give me a second.” Bella broke off from his hold and turned to the kitchen instead of the chairs by the roaring fireplace. “Hey, Em...can I get a couple cups of something warm?”

Emory turned around from her gingerbread house. “Sure. Who for?”

Bella tried to hold her grin in check, but she couldn’t. “Henry and myself.”

Emory smiled back. “He’s spending a lot of time here,” she hedged.

“He’s working on a case.”

Emory’s right eyebrow slowly rose. “Is that the only reason he’s here?”

Taking the tray from Emory’s hands, which contained much more than two cups of cocoa, Emory pumped her own eyebrows. “I sure hope not!” She smiled at Emory’s laugh and headed back out the door.

HANK HELD HIS HANDS over the fire. The warmth slowly began to permeate his skin, leaving sparks of pain in its wake. He grinned as he thought of why he was so cold. Seeing Bella in his large coat, dwarfing her like a little child, had been a sight to behold. He had felt something decidedly possessive about her wearing his clothes, even if it was just an overcoat. It had been an interesting and, frankly, enjoyable sensation.

He liked watching her discover the things he had seen during his investigation. He liked seeing her eyes light up with intelligence. He liked her being his.

That thought caused his brain to stutter to a stop. Enjoying her company and her kisses was one thing. Her being his was another. "One that you're not ready for," he scolded himself.

"Not ready for what?"

Hank spun, heat traveling up his neck. He was grateful he hadn't shaved in a couple of days. *Maybe my beard will cover the blush.* He'd always been irked by his light skin. Since he had blond hair, he was fairer than most of the other men he knew, and it meant endless hours of teasing. He turned red in the sun and blushed when embarrassed. *Nothing about either of those things is impressive. Good thing I live on the coast where we're overcast most of the year.* "Not ready to walk away from the fire," he fibbed, rubbing his hands together. "Emory didn't go to any trouble to make this, did she?"

Bella set the tray on the coffee table and put her hands on her hips. "How do you know I didn't make it?"

A slow grin tugged at his lips. "Because I've seen you take advantage of your cousin's urge to feed people. So unless she's not in the kitchen, you definitely didn't make those..." He looked at the tray and frowned. "What is it?"

Bella gave him a triumphant look. "Not so sure of yourself now, are you?"

Hank stepped closer to her and wrapped his hands around her waist. "I don't know," he murmured. "I'm pretty sure of myself." He ran his nose along her cheek and laughed when she danced away.

"Oh my word, your nose is cold." She picked up a mug and practically shoved it at him. "Here. Warm up."

Hank couldn't help but keep his eyes on her as he took a sip of the hot cider. It was fruity and sweet, but not too sweet. Just how he liked it. But it was Bella's reaction that had him feeling satisfied. Her eyes were locked on his and he wasn't about to let her off that easily.

All her antics and teasing and he hadn't gotten a single kiss yet today. So seeing her squirm at his stare was more than he could have hoped for.

Clearing her throat, Bella finally broke their contest and picked up her own mug, taking a sip, then fanning her tongue. "Wow, that's hot." She eyed him. "How can you drink it?"

He shrugged and held the mug between his cold hands. "Must be a detective thing."

She snorted and picked up one of the cookies he didn't recognize. "Detective, deshmective," she muttered.

"You still didn't tell me what that was," he asked, the smell of vanilla teasing his senses.

Bella waved it at him. "What? Can't your detective skills tell you? Maybe if you take a bite, it'll answer all your questions."

Hank put down his drink and took the two steps to her side. He wrapped his arms around her back, tugging her into his chest. She gave a moment's fight, but he grinned when she settled in fairly easily. "Or maybe I'll just use my resources and ask." He leaned down to her ear. "A good detective always uses his resources."

"And a good journalist always keeps things close to the chest," she answered back breathlessly.

Hank chuckled. "Touche." He looked down at her, then glanced at the cookie she still held aloft. Keeping her eyes, he bent his head and took a bite from her fingers. The texture was definitely something he had not expected. It was more cake-like than cookie-ish. But the sweet vanilla he'd smelled earlier was clearly present and deliciously wonderful. "Mmm..." He took the last piece from her hand. "I don't know what it is, but I want more."

With her hands now empty, Bella put them on his chest. "Too bad. The rest are for me," she shot back. "Especially since you just ate mine."

Hank grinned. She was cute when she thought she'd won. "Then I guess I'll have to take them a different way." Quickly bending down, he kissed her, long and hard. She was much sweeter than any cookie, no matter how delicious it was.

It only took a moment for her arms to wind around his neck and for her to bounce up on tiptoe. It was a move he was coming to recognize in her. She was always eager and her feet told the story. He kissed her a minute longer, knowing he would never get enough, but also knowing he needed to get back to work.

Breaking their kiss, he leaned back just enough to look her in the eye. She felt far too right in his arms, and it worried him a little. Bella was not a permanent part of Seagull Cove. After the New Year, she'd be gone, and he was falling too fast for this to be a good thing.

Letting go of her, he spun, grabbed two of the cookies, and darted back to the fireplace. "Guess these are mine now."

"What!" Bella screeched. She leapt over and tried to take them from his hand, but Hank held them above her head. Her tiny legs just couldn't jump that far, no matter how hard she tried.

Finally, breathing heavily, Bella paused and put her hands on her hips.

Hank didn't even have to look to know her foot was tapping at a hundred miles an hour.

"Fine. Keep the stupid cookies," she huffed, turning and flipping her hair over her shoulder. "See if I care." She plopped onto the couch and Hank couldn't help but follow.

Sitting down beside her, he offered one to her. "A cookie for a name?"

Bella shook her head. "No way. It's too late, detective boy. You lost your chance."

Hank just wiggled it in front of her, and finally Bella grabbed it. "Name," he reminded her.

She ate the cookie and brushed off her fingers and skirt, then shrugged. "I don't know."

"What?" Hank sat back.

She grinned. "You didn't bother to check that I actually had the information you were looking for." Bella tsked her tongue. "That's a rookie move, Sherlock. Better up your game next time."

Scowling at her, Hank ate the other one he'd nabbed. He knew he could just stop and ask Emory on his way out the door, but it was much more fun to play with Bella. Unless he was the one losing, and this time around, he'd lost.

He grinned and shook his head. "Well played, Ms. Wood. Well played."

She gave him a mock salute. "All in a day's work." Bella sighed and put her hands on her lap. "So...now what?"

Hank rubbed his hands on his pants and pulled out his phone. "Now, let's go over what we know and what we're still missing. Sound good?"

Bella squealed and bounced up to kiss his cheek. "Yes! Let me grab my phone!" She ran out of the room, presumably to the front desk, and came hurrying back with phone in hand. "I keep everything on my note app."

Hank waved his phone in the air. "Me too."

Instead of sitting in her own seat, Bella plopped herself on his lap, wiggling around until she was comfortable. "Okay. Now tell me what you've got."

What I've got is a massive crush on a girl who's leaving in a few weeks, Hank thought to himself. *And I'm not sure I'm going to be able to let her go.*

CHAPTER 9

Bella tapped her lips with her pencil. After seeing the crumbs outside the house, she was growing more and more determined to figure out who was taking Emory's food. It was disappearing with alarming regularity. She was tempted to go back to the attic room, but Henry had already cleared everything out of there, so Bella was fairly sure the intruder wouldn't be stupid enough to stick around.

"But they have to be somewhere," she mused. "Otherwise, the food wouldn't keep being stolen." She squished her lips to the side. "But where?"

The garden shed popped into her mind again. True, the crumbs had been found just outside the door, but a garden rake had been left in the grass at one point and nobody could figure out how.

"Plus, the shed isn't very far from the door they used," Bella said firmly. Checking the clock, she transferred the phone line again to her cell and headed to the coat closet to grab her jacket. This Oregon Coast weather was no joke. It might not get as low in temperature as other places, but the wet and windy conditions made it pretty miserable nonetheless.

After bundling up, she headed out the side door. "Geez." Bella pulled the collar of her coat tighter around her throat. Putting her head down, she marched on, determined to see what was going on at the shed. Enoch had said it was locked up tight, but Bella wanted to know for herself.

She headed straight for the doors, and sure enough, a padlock hung between the two swinging doors. Bella tugged on it, but it was firm and secure, just as it should be. She huffed and put her hands on her hips, tapping her foot rapidly. "There's got to be a clue here."

Search as she might, Bella couldn't find any way that a thief would be able to get into the garden shed. It seemed nearly impenetrable, save the small window, which was too high for her to get a good look at.

She pursed her lips and looked around. The glass was clearly unbroken, but maybe someone could shimmy through if they were tall enough? Which Bella was definitely not. Finally she found a stack of wood, which had been used for the fireplaces before gas had been installed a few years back.

Grabbing the largest piece she could find, Bella drug it over and turned it on its end. Inching her pencil skirt up her thighs slightly, she stepped onto the log, teetering slightly in her high heels. "Whoa." She pressed a hand to the side of the shed to keep herself steady, then turned her body toward the window.

It took raising up on tiptoe in order for her to see through the window, but the interior was dark and the window dusty, making her efforts worth little.

Using the side of her hand, Bella rubbed at the glass, hoping to make it a little clearer, but there was too much dirt on the inside as well. Huffing, she leaned in, pressing her face to the pane and focusing on anything she could actually see. The outline of the lawnmower was easy to pick out, but the rest was mostly in shadow. "Somehow I'm gonna have to wrangle up the key to this place—"

"What the he—?"

"Ahhh!" Bella screamed, tottering in her heels. It wasn't that far to the ground, she knew, but in her heels and skirt, she was afraid she would twist an ankle or something.

"Of all the idiotic..." Henry's voice trailed off as he plucked her off the log before she could fall and planted her safely on the ground.

Bella put her hand to her chest, taking in large gulps of air and thanking her lucky stars for strong men. "Holy cow. That was close." After getting her breath back, she turned to Henry and scowled. "What do you mean, coming up and scaring me like that!"

Henry jerked back. "What do *I* mean? Why am I the one in trouble here? I think the problem was the fact that you were peering into a window while standing on a log in a skirt and *heels*! What were you thinking?" He folded his arms over his broad chest. Bella had to keep her eyes from straying to the thick muscles he was using to intimidate her.

It was not in her nature to be cowed, especially when she'd done nothing wrong. She brushed down her skirt, which had risen even higher in the debacle, and sniffed. "I was doing some detective work, if you must know. I don't see how what I'm wearing has anything to do with it."

"It does when it could send you to the hospital," he growled back. "And I thought we were supposed to do this together. Why are you sleuthing around without me?"

Bella rolled her eyes. "Are you telling me I can't even walk around my own family property without you by my side?"

"If you're looking for evidence, then yes."

Bella ground her teeth. "That kind of attitude right there is exactly why I haven't been able to break into this business," she spit out. "It's men like you who think that women have no place doing anything remotely dangerous, and I'm sick of it!" She stomped her foot, which only made her heel sink into the dirt rather than give the satisfying crack she was hoping for.

Henry pointed a finger at her. "I have no problem with women being in my workforce," he argued. "And you should know that by the fact that I've let you help out on this little investigation. Where I have an issue is untrained people going off without any thought in their heads except for some delusion of grandeur at solving a case, and getting themselves hurt or in trouble, because they think they're some kind of Nancy Drew or part of the Scooby Doo gang."

Bella didn't know when she'd ever been so mad. Henry had basically just called her an idiot. He'd lumped her in with every yahoo who'd ever watched an episode of CSI and thought that made them an expert.

Well, she wasn't someone like that. She'd been to school for journalism, and she'd studied those who had gone before her. Was she a little too eager? Probably, but that was a natural part of her nature and curiosity. There was nothing wrong with ambition.

She'd fought bullies in her career before, but hearing those words from Henry's lips were harder. She had started to fall for him. His kisses were addicting and his protectiveness was swoonworthy. Except when it wasn't. And right now...it definitely wasn't. There was nothing wrong with what she'd been doing. A little sprained ankle wasn't going to kill anyone or send them to the hospital.

She wanted to keep fighting, to put him in his place, but her eyes were starting to sting, and she knew tears were imminent. For one of the very few times in her life, Bella had nothing to say. Spinning on her heel, she marched away from Henry, determined not to let him see how much he'd hurt her.

HANK'S KNEES NEARLY gave out as he watched Bella walk away from him. He'd seen the sheen of water in her eyes before she'd stuck her chin in the air and walked away like the proud woman she was. He'd put that sheen there. He'd been the one to make her cry, and it made him feel lower than the dirt under his shoes.

He blew out a breath and scrubbed his face with his cold hands. "That did *not* go well." He sighed. He'd overreacted. He knew he had. But what was a man to do? He'd been able to see her from the driveway, standing on a log of all things, in her tight skirt and high heels, trying to look into a shed window. The fear of her falling and breaking a leg or hitting her head on something had grasped him so tightly, Hank had hardly been able to breathe. "Why the heck didn't she just get the key?" he muttered.

He watched her round the corner of the house, headed for the front door. "And why is she going in the front?" *To get away from you, idiot.*

Hank nodded at his inner voice. That was most likely correct. She could have just walked to the side door, but that wouldn't have been a dramatic enough exit.

"AHHH!"

Hank's eyes widened at the scream and he immediately rushed around the house. Instead of the danger he'd thought he'd encounter, Hank found Bella sprawled on the concrete walkway. She was lying on her back with her eyes closed, making Hank slow down his approach. "Belle?" he asked cautiously. "What happened?"

"Oh, nothing," she answered, her voice strong, which allowed his muscles to relax from their tension. "I just like to hang out on icy sidewalks where anybody and everybody can step on me."

"Icy?" Hank frowned and came closer, keeping an eye on her. As he approached the edge of the concrete, he stopped. Sure enough, there was a definite glisten to the walkway. He put his foot out and tested the area. "Wow, that's slippery."

"No kidding, Sherlock."

Hank bit back a grin at her response. She was livid at him, and Hank knew he needed to apologize, but right now things were just a little on the humorous side. He put his hands on his hips. "So...are you hurt?"

She opened those sky blue eyes and they nearly impaled him with their anger. "I don't know. Why don't you figure it out? After all, I'm just a woman. How can I tell these things?"

Hank sighed and pinched the bridge of his nose. "Belle, surely you can see—"

She scrambled to her feet, slipping and sliding on the sidewalk, but managing to get upright. "No, I cannot see. What I see is a caveman who doesn't know how to come into the twenty-first century." She threw her arms wide, slipping a little more. "Well, welcome Detective Gordon. We women are here, and we plan to stay. We can hold any job we want and there's nothing you can do to stop it."

Hank held out his hand in a conciliatory manner. "Belle, you know that wasn't it, sweetheart."

"Don't call me that," she said, her voice having gone low and dark.

The tears were back and Hank once again felt like a worm. "Isabella," he said softly, gaining her attention. "I'm sorry."

She blinked at him. "What?"

"I said, I'm sorry."

Her bottom lip began to tremble. "That real question is, do you know what you're sorry for?"

Staying on the grass, which wasn't slippery at all, Hank reached out and took her arm, sliding her his way until they were both stable. Then he wrapped his arms around her back and brought her into his chest. "I'm sorry I scared you on the log." He could feel her stiffen and he hurried to continue before she snapped at him again. "I'm sorry I yelled at you. I'm sorry I spoke harshly to you. I'm sorry I made you feel like you didn't belong in this type of work."

She sniffled and buried her face in his coat. "That's a start, I suppose," she said thickly.

Hank smiled softly and shook his head, his hands rubbing up and down her wet coat. "The truth is, seeing you in a dangerous position scared me," he finally admitted. He wasn't normally one to admit his feelings about anything, but this dramatic little spitfire in his arms was changing all sorts of things about him. And he wasn't exactly regretting it, which surprised him more than anything. "It made me say things that I shouldn't." Cupping her face, he pulled her back. "Can you forgive me?"

Bella nodded. "Yes, as long as you realize how stupid you were."

Hank chuckled and kissed the end of her cold, red nose. "I do."

She pulled out of his hold. “Good. Because your hands are freezing and I want to go inside.” She turned back to the sidewalk, then paused. “And I’m sorry for calling you a caveman.”

Hank wrapped his arms around her from behind and pulled her back into his body. “Is that all?”

“I might have called you a few more bad names in my head,” she admitted sheepishly.

He held back the urge to roll his eyes. “Annnd...” he pressed.

“And next time, I’ll make sure there’s no ice when I walk on the sidewalk.”

“Bella...” he warned.

She sighed and threw up her arms, looking over her shoulder at him. “I won’t promise not to go looking for clues, Henry. It’s just not going to happen.”

He sighed. “Will you at least promise to do it in sneakers and pants next time?”

She grinned. “Maybe. But don’t tell me you didn’t enjoy the show. I know these heels make my legs look good. Why do you think I wear them?”

Heat began to run up his neck and the cold wind had no affect on him at all for a moment. Clearing his throat, Hank let her go and scratched at his beard. “I think I’ll plead the fifth on that one.”

Bella laughed, then turned back to the sidewalk. “That problem might be fixed, but what about this one?” She toed the ice. “I don’t know why we would have such an icy sidewalk. Enoch usually puts out ice melt if there’s a storm coming.”

Hank cursed at himself in his head. He’d been so focused on calming Bella down, he hadn’t thought about how unusual it would be for the sidewalk to be so slick. *You’re losing your touch, old man,* he scolded himself. *And all because of a woman.*

CHAPTER 10

Bella put her hands on her hips and tapped her foot. "This isn't right." She could feel Henry's strong presence close behind her.

"I agree." He grunted. "In fact, I think it looks like someone intentionally poured water over the whole of it."

Bella let her eyes trail over the ice. "I think you might be right. But why?" She turned to meet his dark eyes. "I thought we were after a food thief. How does this fit in?"

Henry tore his hat off his head and pushed a hand through his hair before replacing it. "I have no idea."

Staying on the grass, Bella walked up to the front porch and carefully made her way up the steps. "Enoch keeps the ice melt over here in the corner. I think we need to lay some out."

"Let me help," Henry said, jumping up the steps to her side.

Not that she would ever admit it, but the bags were fifty pounds each, and Bella was grateful for Henry's help. He lifted the bag as if it weighed nothing, which only made him more impressive in her eyes.

She had been so angry at him, feeling like the man who was weaseling his way under her skin was just like everyone else. And then he had to go and admit he was wrong and that he had been worried for her. What was a girl supposed to do against an assault like that?

Be magnanimous enough to forgive, and then make sure you tease him about it, she thought to herself with a chuckle.

"I think that's about it," Henry murmured. He looked at her. "What do you think? Did we miss any?"

Bella realized that while she was daydreaming, Henry had taken care of it all. The entire sidewalk was now covered in tiny pebbles and the ice was clearly melting underneath the onslaught of chemicals.

"Wow. Good work, Sherlock." She laughed when Henry gave her a dry look.

"I'm gonna have to put my foot down about that nickname," he said, bringing the bag back to the corner of the porch.

"Awww..." Bella teased. "Why? I think it fits you perfectly." She grinned as he stormed her way. Once he was within reach, she fixed his lapel and patted his chest. "I'm not sure I can ever go back to anything else."

Henry's expression didn't change. "If you actually meant it as a compliment, it wouldn't be so bad."

Bella laughed again and slid her hands up his chest. "I'm sorry. It was mean of me." She dropped her voice. "Whatever can I do to make it up to you?"

Henry's eyes seemed to darken to a deep smolder and Bella's pulse leapt. Oh, how she adored kissing this man. He had the ability to make her feel beautiful, cherished, and desirable all from a single touch. And now, after their fight, seemed like the perfect time for a little make-up session.

"I'm pretty sure I can think of something," he whispered as his head descended.

A shrill scream, heavily muffled, rang through the air.

"What the heck?" Bella breathed, breaking away from his hold. "I think that came from inside." She turned to the door, but Henry had beaten her to it. She rushed after him, her heels clicking on the hardwood floor as soon as she got inside.

Henry had stopped in the front entry and was turning in a circle. "Where did it come from?" he asked, his voice low.

Bella shook her head. "No idea." She shucked her coat and threw it to the side, keeping her ears peeled. "Here. Let me take your coat."

"I'm not worried about my coat," Henry ground out.

"Well, until you know where you're going, we might as well wait a second," Bella shot back.

With a growl, Henry tore off his coat and threw it to the side. It skidded across the floor and Bella tsked her tongue.

A crash came from further into the house and both of them jumped as if they'd been electrocuted.

"The display room," Bella said breathlessly, her heart sinking. "If there's been another accident, Emory is going to have a breakdown. She already had to remake an entire wal. There's no time in the schedule for anything more. The displays are due to come in tomorrow."

Henry took off and Bella hurried after him. They rushed down the hall toward the room, only to see Emory standing still in the hallway. She put up her hand and Bella forced herself to slow down.

Emory's face was one of disbelief. As if she couldn't quite believe what was happening. She backed up a few steps, turned to look in the open doorway, and her shoulders crumpled.

Bella hurried up and peered around her cousin. Antony was in the room, squatting low on his heels, peering into a pile of wreckage. Bella felt her jaw drop as she took in the destroyed room. Tables and decorations were thrown everywhere, and some of the tables appeared to have been smashed in half. "What is going on?" Bella breathed.

"I think everyone should stay back," Emory said, the sadness in her tone clearly audible.

"Let me in, Emory," Henry said firmly, but kindly.

With a slow nod, Emory turned, leaving room for Henry to enter and walk across the room to Antony. Just as he went to go inside, Emory darted into the room and got on her knees next to Antony.

"It's a boy!" Emory exclaimed in surprise.

Bella tried to speed up and follow, but Henry put out his arm and held her back. They walked slowly across the room to where the other adults were gathered.

"Jim Harmon," Antony was saying to Emory. "I think we found our food thief."

"Emory, what's going on under there?" Henry asked, his voice hinting of impatience.

Bella could practically feel the anxiety pouring off of him. His entire body was tight with tension and his arm was like steel where it kept her from moving past him.

Emory looked up, sighed, and rose to her feet. "Antony thinks he found our thief." She stepped out of the way and Henry moved in to take her place. Antony also scooted sideways.

Bella watched with mounting anticipation as she saw Henry get down and push his baseball cap back off his forehead. "What do we have here?" he mused. "Mind telling me your name, son?"

"I'm not your son."

Ooh, we've got a live one, Bella thought with a quiet chuckle. She threaded her arm through Emory's and prepared to wait for more answers.

HANK'S HEART WAS BEING squeezed from the inside out. He recognized the obstinate but helpless look in the boy's eyes. His thin frame was dwarfed by the black hoodie he wore, and he looked and smelled as if he hadn't bathed in weeks. "That might be, but I'd still like to know your name," Hank pressed.

The young teenager pinched his lips together, his dark eyes judging Hank. "Jim. And I already told that guy." Jim thrust his chin toward Antony.

"Can you tell me where your parents are?" Hank asked as kindly as possible. He didn't normally deal with runaways, but for this boy to be in this kind of shape, his home situation had to be bad.

"I don't have any."

"Everyone has parents, Jim, even if they don't like them," Hank said with a small smile. He kept hoping if he stayed calm the boy would relax a little, but so far it wasn't working.

"Not everyone. Orphans don't have parents," Jim ground out.

"Are you an orphan?"

A mulish look crossed Jim's face and he turned away, refusing to answer. Which meant that Hank had all the answers he needed. He sighed and rubbed the bridge of his nose. This was becoming more complicated than he'd expected.

A body crawled past him and Hank looked over, startled. "Bella," he warned, watching her maneuver her way through the destroyed table Jim had taken refuge under.

"Lay off, big guy," she snipped back. "This guy needs a hug, and I aim to give it to him."

Jim's eyes were wide, though Hank couldn't help but see the hope in them. He climbed to his feet just as Bella's arms surrounded the kid and hugged him tight. "I'm gonna kill her," he muttered, rubbing the edge of his jaw. She was so stubborn. He glanced at the table. And yet so wonderful. What other woman of his acquaintance would be willing to crawl on the floor in a skirt and blouse, work their way through a destroyed table, and hug a smelly teenage boy just because he was struggling?

A headache began to form behind his eyes. *Why do I have the feeling that my life will never be the same now? This tiny blip of a woman has completely upended me and I'm not running for the hills. I must be a glutton for punishment.*

Only a few minutes later, Bella and Jim came crawling out.

"Emory?" Bella asked, completely ignoring Hank. "Jim here needs a cookie and a glass of milk." Bella smiled and put her arm around his thin shoulders. "Think you can help us out?"

Emory seemed to be considering the situation for a moment before shaking her head. "No..." she started, causing Bella to shoot her a look. "I actually don't have any warm cookies at the moment." She smiled. "But I do have some scones. They're chocolate chip," she added.

Jim frowned. "What's a scone?"

"You've never had a scone?" Bella asked in fake horror. She put a hand on her chest and began to walk the boy toward the kitchen door. "They're only the best things ever!" She leaned in conspiratorially. "They're like a mix between a biscuit and cookie." Her voice trailed off as they disappeared into the kitchen.

Hank shook his head but didn't follow. He needed a minute to get his head on straight. Bella's compassion but fiery attitude was killing him. He needed to get her out of his head and put it back on the case. But how? She was everywhere. And now she had his suspect in the kitchen and was feeding him scones and milk.

He turned when Antony and Emory murmured to each other. Emory's eyes were filled with tears, but she straightened her shoulders, thrust her chin in the air, and marched into the kitchen after her cousin.

Antony's intense stare told Hank that the baker was just as involved with Emory as Hank was with Bella. Apparently this family raised impressive females. Emory's entire display room for the festival had just been destroyed, and instead of being angry or throwing a tantrum, she'd gone right along with Bella and was feeding a criminal.

"She's quite something," Hank said, coming to Antony's side.

Antony nodded. "She is."

"And a bit less stubborn than her cousin," Hank grumbled.

Antony chuckled and stuffed his hands in his pockets. "I doubt it," he said. "She just might be less...prone to waving it in people's faces."

Hank nodded reluctantly. That was probably truer than he wanted it to be. A woman who could become as good as Emory at baking had to have a backbone of steel. But he also had to reluctantly admit that it was Bella's outspoken nature and witty banter that kept Hank coming back for more, despite her tendency toward rashness.

Grumbling under his breath, he headed into the kitchen to find the entire household of women standing around a very proud Jim Harmon as he stuffed his face full of food. They looked up at him as he entered and Hank had a sneaking suspicion he had just become the enemy.

Crud. This is not what I needed in my life.

Hank smiled to break the tension. "I think he eats better than I do," he quipped, folding his arms over his chest.

All the women looked his way with varying degrees of surprise. "If you'd barely been eating enough to live on for the last four months, you might get a good meal and some sympathy too," Bella sniffed. She ran a hand over the boy's head, smiling at him. "Fill your belly and then we'll get you all cleaned up, okay?"

"Now hold on," Hank said, grabbing a chair and turning it backward so he could straddle it. He sat down across from the kid. "We need to have a chat," he stated firmly, but not unkindly. Antony stepped up behind Hank and he was grateful for his support. *At least someone sees sense here.*

"Careful, Hank," Bella said in a warning tone

"I have to do my job, Belle," he said softly. "That's what I'm here for."

She sighed. "I know, but just...go easy on him, huh?"

Hank nodded his understanding. He didn't want to hurt the boy, he just wanted answers. The next fifteen minutes were spent doing just that, but Hank came away with less than he had before. Jim had run away from a bad foster situation from a town down the road. He'd been hiding in the attic and sneaking food to survive, but had gotten caught today. The worst part had come when he'd admitted to seeing someone destroy the display room with a sledgehammer, but the man ran away before anyone else could see him.

Mrs. Harrison, who had joined in the conversation in the middle, took Jim and marched him over to the kitchen. She began to give him orders and seemed to be teaching him how to cook a meal.

"What the..." Bella had come up to stand by Emory. "I can't believe it. There is a soft side to the drama queen." She looked over and smiled. "No offense, Antony."

"None taken," he said from Emory's side. "It's fine. I know Mother has a passionate side. But she's also a good mother. I mean, she raised seven children. She knows what she's doing."

"Seven?" Emory gasped. "You never told me that."

"Let me guess...you're the youngest," Bella added.

Antony laughed. "Guilty as charged."

"Speaking of guilty," Hank said, standing up and joining in their little pow-wow. "I don't know what to do with the kid." He shook his head. "I'll have to call the social worker in charge of him, but I'm not sure how to handle the stealing."

"I don't want to press charges," Emory said quickly.

Hank raised an eyebrow. "None?" He nodded when Emory shook her head with conviction. *Okay...no charges. But we've still got to get the kid back to where he belongs. And I have to do it without upsetting Bella.*

CHAPTER 11

Bella's heart went out to her cousin as Emory began to quietly cry. Everything she had worked so hard for was falling apart, and yet no one could bring themselves to do anything about it because it was a young boy who was in a bad situation.

Nobody is that heartless, she thought glumly. *But what about Emory? She shouldn't lose everything either. It's not fair.*

Antony was suggesting they rebuild and Bella perked up. It would be a massive undertaking, but it could be done.

"I should go get Enoch," Hope said from behind them, then rushed from the room.

"No, don't..." Emory deflated against Antony. "Rebuilding it would take all night. There's no way I can ask you guys to do that."

"You're not asking," Bella said firmly. "We're offering." She turned and gave Henry her best smile. "Aren't we, Henry?"

Henry's eyebrows went up. "You sure you want me with a hammer? While I'm happy to pitch in somewhere, I'm pretty sure I'll only end up with bruised thumbs if I try to build something."

He's not getting out of this that easily. Bella tapped her bottom lip. "I've always had a thing for a man in a tool belt. Maybe I should go help Hope find Enoch."

Henry scowled at her. "Really? That's how you want to play this?"

Bella opened her eyes wide, knowing she looked innocent and young when she did. "Play what? This isn't a game."

Henry rolled his eyes and huffed. "You, woman, are impossible."

"Thank you!" Bella chirped. She latched onto his arm and jumped in order to give him a kiss on the cheek. "I'll make sure it's worth your time," she whispered in his ear.

Henry stiffened, then looked down at her, his eyes smoldering. "Oh, really?"

Bella winked. "Yep."

He sighed. "Then I suppose having two black thumbs will be worth it."

Bella laughed, still hanging on his arm. "Come on, Tim The Tool Man Taylor. Let's get this party started."

Henry grumbled, but followed her into the display room. Bella took a deep breath. She was all for helping her cousin and the inn, but this was going to be one heck of a project. "What do we do first?" she muttered.

"Start by taking out all the garbage," Enoch offered from the doorway.

Bella turned to him and waved, grinning. "Nice tool belt," she said, looking slyly at Henry.

His glare could have melted the royal frosting of Emory's gingerbread house. "I'm starting to wonder why I put up with this," he grumbled.

Bella sobered and took his hand, leading Henry to the far corner where they had a moment's privacy. Guilt was slithering through her chest. She knew she was a tease, and the bantering and flirting that ensued was one of her favorite things in the world. Bella had found many years ago that if she wasn't intellectually stimulated, she was quick to boredom, and that sometimes led to stupid decisions.

However, she'd also learned that people had a breaking point. And she found herself truly not wanting to cross Henry's. He was amazing. Not only in his looks, but his compassion, his protectiveness, his sharp mind, and even his gruffness. She adored all those parts of him. So, hearing him say he was tired of her teasing had hurt, but was a clear signal she was going too far.

She swallowed her pride, as large and difficult as it was, and forced herself to speak. "I'm sorry."

Henry looked taken aback. "What?"

Bella deflated, her eyes dropping from his as she stared at the ground. "I'm sorry, Henry." She peered up from under her lashes. "I like to tease, but your comment made me realize I was going too far." Her hands came together in front of her. "You know I'm not interested in Enoch, right?"

Henry nodded. "Yeah, I know that. You're not the type to encroach on your cousin's claim."

Bella rolled her eyes. "While I'm glad you know I wouldn't do that, I also just have no interest in Enoch." She shrugged. "He's nice enough, but not anywhere near what I'm looking for."

Henry's smile was slow and enticing. "Oh? Just what are you looking for?"

Bella began to draw swirls on his chest. "Someone tall."

"Enoch isn't exactly short."

"Someone handsome."

"Most women would probably call him that as well."

Bella gave him a look. "Someone with dark eyes."

Henry's blond eyebrow rose high. "That's pretty darn specific."

"Someone who keeps me on my toes."

He glanced down. "That isn't hard. You're always on your toes because you can't reach anything otherwise."

Bella frowned and slapped his chest. "Jerk."

Henry laughed and grabbed her hand. "Sorry. I couldn't resist."

Bella tugged on her hand halfheartedly. "I don't think you're very sorry. And all after I apologized to you."

Henry was still laughing as he put his arms around her back and brought her in close. "You're right. I'm not very sorry." He grinned and kissed the end of her nose. "And I do appreciate your apology. You're feisty and fun, traits that I enjoy, but no man wants to be told his girl is interested in someone else."

"But I'm not—" she started to argue.

"I know you're not, but you were still talking about it."

Bella huffed. "Sorry. I won't tease you about that again."

He kissed the top of her head. "I appreciate it. Thank you." Henry turned and surveyed the room. "Now...should we jump in and get going?"

Bella leaned into his side and took a deep breath. "I suppose we should, but I have to admit I'd rather be cuddled up with you, exchanging notes."

Henry chuckled and she bounced against him. "Yeah...this isn't my scene either, but your cousin needs our help, and if I've learned anything about you, it's that you're fiercely loyal to your loved ones."

"And don't you forget it," she quipped.

"Never." After one last kiss to the top of her head, Henry pushed her forward and the two of them began to pick up pieces of wood and drag them outside.

"Such a waste," Bella said softly as she dumped yet another broken sheet of plywood. She looked around and frowned. "Where did Enoch go?"

"He's picking up new supplies," Hope offered, wiping her dusty hands on her pants. "The store is two towns over and Enoch happens to know the owner, so he's hoping to trade in a favor."

"I haven't even thought of that," Bella said softly. She shook her head. "Geez, this is turning out to be way more extensive than I thought."

"And we still need to figure out why the ice was on the walkway," Henry said in an aside as he walked by.

"Oh my word, I almost forgot about all that," Bella said in exasperation. "I was too caught up in Jimmy."

HANK NODDED SOLEMNLY. "It's easy to get caught up in the moment," he agreed. "What I'm most concerned about, however, is the man Jim said destroyed the room. If we can catch him, then I think we've solved the whole case."

Bella grinned. "You sound like a TV cop."

Hank closed his eyes and chuckled. "You would only know that if you watch them."

She shrugged a shoulder. "So what if I do? Crimes fascinate me. I watch all the documentaries too."

"How are you with horror movies?"

Bella blew a raspberry and waved a hand in the air. "Haven't found one to frighten me yet."

"Wow." He nodded, his lips pursed. "That's impressive. I would never have guessed someone like you would be so thick-skinned."

Bella scowled and put her hands on her hips, her foot tapping as per the norm. "What do you mean, someone like me?"

Hank laughed and took her hand, leading her back to the work zone. "Someone who looks like they'd never hurt a fly. I'm learning you have a sadistic streak, and it's throwing me off kilter."

"If you can't handle the heat, get out of the kitchen," she shot back.

Hank squeezed her hand before letting go. "Oh, I can handle it," he said, then leaned in for a second. "In fact, I do believe I've been the one to start the fire a few times." He grinned when her cheeks turned bright pink. It wasn't exactly easy to make Bella blush, but when it happened, it was a sight to behold.

"I think maybe I should go work over here," she said breathlessly, pointing to the opposite side of the room.

He watched her fan herself as she walked away and couldn't help but laugh. The woman was brash, overeager, and sometimes teased a little too much, but she was also compassionate, loyal, fun, and quickly capturing his heart. He loved her dedication to truth and willingness to work. He also loved her snappy comebacks and how she kept their relationship interesting and lively. *I do believe I'm on the way to losing my whole heart, and I'm not sure how, or if I want, to stop it.*

He forced the thoughts to the back of his mind. That was a case for another day. Right now he needed to figure out why there was still a mystery left at Gingerbread Inn and help get a festival back on its feet. That was more than enough for one man to handle.

By the time they had finished rebuilding the display room, the sun was rising on the horizon and Hank felt as if his body had been hit by a Mac truck. He groaned as he climbed to his feet after pushing the last screw into place.

"I think that's it!" Bella cried, bouncing on her toes.

Right now Hank envied her ability to have such energy. He was beat. It seemed that each time he pulled an all-nighter, they got harder and harder. *How the heck did I do so many of them during college?* he mused.

"You going home?" Bella asked. If he hadn't been looking closely, Hank would never have noticed the dark circles forming under her eyes. It made him feel better to know that she was just as susceptible to exhaustion as he was, though she hid it better.

"Yeah...I think I might try to get a few hours of sleep under my belt before picking things back up later today."

"You're coming to the festival though, right?"

Hank nodded, a yawn keeping him from speaking. "I need to find Jim's social worker, then I should be able to enjoy the festivities better."

Bella nodded. "Good luck with that."

Hank shrugged. "It'll be easier than it sounds. He told us what town he's from. It shouldn't be too hard to figure out who's in charge and ask if they're missing a child." Hank scratched at his chin. "Truth be told, I'm surprised something didn't come through our announcements. A missing kid should be pretty big news, and would have been spread through most of the state."

Bella shrugged. "I have no idea how it all works."

"Me either," Hank admitted. "This is outside my normal jurisdiction." He sighed, his body feeling like it was weighed down by concrete blocks. "Maybe something did come through and I just didn't see it."

Bella took his hand and began walking. "Well, it doesn't really matter. What's important is that you go home and get some sleep and then come back tonight, so I can fill you with sugar and cinnamon that Emory cooked to perfection."

Hank laughed as she led him to the front door. "I find it amazing that you never offer me your own baked goods. Only your cousin's."

Bella gave him a crooked grin. "What would you say if I told you I can't cook to save my life?"

Hank slowly shook his head and tugged her back to kiss her forehead. "I'd say I'm not surprised. It seems to fit everything else I'm learning about you."

"Hey!" Bella smacked his arm.

Hank laughed, feeling a little more awake then he'd been a moment before. Bella had that effect on him. She just exuded life and energy. "I didn't say it was a bad thing," he responded. "I just said it fits the package."

She huffed. "Well, it doesn't sound like a compliment."

"Don't worry," Hank said as he grabbed the door handle. "If I was interested in a cook, I would never have taken you on a date to begin with."

Bella rolled her eyes. "Good to know."

Hank was still smiling as he opened the door and began to step outside.

"Wait!"

He paused and then blinked as his eyes registered something on the front step.

"That was close," Bella said ,stepping around him and picking up the shovel that was right in front of the door. If Hank hadn't quit moving, he'd have stepped right on it and probably gotten hurt. "How did this get here?" She looked up at Hank. "We didn't leave it out when we spread the ice melt, did we?"

Hank shook his head and grabbed a glove out of his pocket. "Can I have that please?"

Bella's eyes widened as she realized what he was doing. "Crud. Now my fingerprints are on it," she whispered.

Hank held back a smile at her dropped tone. "It's okay to speak," he teased. "The shovel can't hear you."

Bella growled a little. "This isn't funny."

"Well, it was kind of funny," Hank admitted, "but I'll keep it to myself." He examined the shovel. "We didn't use a shovel," he murmured. "Someone left it there. But who? And why?"

"The same person who wanted us to fall on the ice," Bella said angrily. "Why are they so intent on hurting someone? And who are they trying to hurt?" Her eyes widened. "Are they after me? Trisha was after Hope, Jim was stealing Emory's things, so that only leaves me. But why would someone be trying to hurt me?"

Hank pinched his lips together, his mind racing. "Can you tell me exactly how your grandmother fell and broke her hip?"

Bella's mouth formed a perfect O. "You've got to be kidding me," she breathed.

"How, Bella?"

"She tripped over a towel that was wadded up in the hallway outside her room."

"Is it normal to find towels on the floor around here?" Hank's tiredness was gone and his eyes darted around the foyer. Everything was spic and span, absolutely no sign of neglect.

"No way," Bella said, her voice slightly shaky. "Grandma always made sure the place was spotless."

"Hmm..."

"That's it? Hmm?" Bella's foot began tapping.

Hank wasn't quite ready to share his suspicions yet. Leaning down, he gave her a quick kiss. "I'll see you at the festival."

"You better have more than a quick kiss for me later!" she called after him.

"You better believe it!" he called back. He knew he'd never get to sleep now. His mind was too awake, and the possibilities too many. If luck was on his side, he just might be able to wrap up the situation at Gingerbread Inn before it ruined Christmas or someone got hurt.

CHAPTER 12

"Welcome to Gingerbread Inn," Bella said for what seemed the millionth time that night. She plastered a smile on her face, took the group's coats, and told them how to get to the display room.

It seemed as if the whole town had come out for the festival. Not that Bella could blame them. She'd seen Emory's show piece and most of the others as they'd come through the inn, and it was amazing to see what people could accomplish.

As long as those people aren't you, she thought with a snort. Bella didn't have a creative bone in her body, but she'd grown to where that didn't bother her much anymore. She had other talents. "I think," she muttered.

"You think what?"

Bella spun and smiled widely. "Why, Jimmy Harmon. Don't you look like a man." She put her hands on her hips. The young boy had cleaned up quite well after Grandma and Mrs. Harrison had gotten ahold of him.

The young man rolled his eyes and pushed his hair out of his face. "You didn't answer my question. And I'm already a man."

Bella bit back her laugh. This kid had moxie. She liked it. "I was just talking to myself."

"About?'

Bella's eyebrows rose up. "My...aren't we nosy?"

"Asked the woman who wants to be a journalist," he shot back.

Bella laughed and wrapped her arm around his shoulders. Even at twelve, he was as tall as she was. "Good point," she conceded.

Bella..." he whined. "Why are you avoiding the question?"

"Why are you so intent on knowing?" she retorted.

"Because I need something to distract me from the adults in there," he said, jamming a thumb over his shoulder. "They're all so serious. I mean, it's gingerbread. Why is everyone making such a big deal out of it?"

"Why?" Bella made a shocked face. "Have you seen what some of those artists have done with their displays?" She shook her head. "Don't you find that kind of skill amazing?"

Jim shrugged. "Nah. Why waste all that time on something you're just going to eat? They spent what? Like, hours creating something pretty that the rest of us will just eat in two minutes."

"You can't eat it," Bella said.

Jimmy's jaw dropped open. "What?"

"Uh...nope." Bella pursed her lips. "They use construction-grade gingerbread, which is hard as a rock. And the royal icing isn't something you want to eat either. It's meant to resemble concrete, not food."

"Are you telling me that they're just going to..." Jimmy's eyes jumped all over the room as he searched for the word he wanted, "to...throw away all that candy and stuff when this is over?"

Bella nodded, her head tilted to the side. "Yeah. You really didn't know that?"

His hands flew up in the air. "Then why the heck did they do this in the first place?"

"Because it's pretty?"

"Who cares!"

Bella smiled and shook her head. "Okay...let's throw this in another direction. Who cares if a grown man can put a ball in a hoop a few feet over his head?"

Jimmy grew serious and put his hands in the air in front of him. "Whoa now. You're crossing a line."

She folded her arms over her chest. "Well, maybe you crossed one when you made fun of the gingerbread houses."

The front door opened just as Jimmy was rolling his eyes, drawing Bella's attention. She hurried over, then paused and drank in the sight. "Well, hello, Sherlock," she quipped.

Henry gave her that smoldering look that she loved so much.

I can't believe I just used that word. She let it float in her head, tasting it in her mind. But there was no other word for it. She loved that look on him. She loved when he came around. She loved bantering with him. In fact, she just plain loved him. *What rotten timing. Who falls in love in the middle of an unsolved case?*

"Hello, Belle," he said, his voice low and husky.

The sound of it sent a little thrill up her spine.

"You look fantastic."

Bella smiled and swished her dress from side to side. She'd chosen a light blue dress that showed off her eyes and figure to its best advantage. And right now she was getting the exact reaction she had hoped for. "You look pretty delicious yourself," she murmured back.

She'd never seen him in a suit, and this one looked like it had been sewn just for him. It spread perfectly across his shoulders and chest, the dark blue color making his deep brown eyes look fathomless.

"Oh, brother."

Bella grinned. She'd forgotten Jimmy was in the foyer with her.

"Delicious? Really?" Jimmy groaned. "Maybe as delicious as those inedible gingerbread houses."

Bella snorted as she tried to hold back her laughter.

Henry's right eyebrow rose. "What's he talking about?"

"Oh, nothing," Bella sang. "We were just discussing which was more ridiculous. Gingerbread competitions or basketball."

"Sounds serious."

"Oh, it was," Bella assured him.

"Basketball isn't ridiculous," Jimmy said forcefully. "Building food you can't eat is."

Bella turned back to the young teenager. "If you say so."

"Whatever." He rolled his eyes again in true teenage fashion. "I'm going back inside."

"Don't you dare eat anyone's display," Bella called after him.

"Yeah, yeah."

"Nice kid."

Henry's voice was right behind her and Bella's heart skipped a beat, then picked up speed. Whether from his nearness or from startling her, she couldn't quite tell. Slowly, she spun to face him, tilting her head way back to look him in the eye. "He can be. But like most teenage boys, he doesn't see the point in art...or food he can't consume."

Henry nodded slowly, his eyes fixed on her lips. "I see."

"You didn't hear anything I said, did you?" she asked with a grin.

He shook his head. "Nope. I'm afraid my mind was on something else."

"Would it have to do with the mistletoe hanging over us?" Bella asked, her voice growing breathless in anticipation.

"It didn't, but since you gave me the excuse..."

THE LAST TWO DAYS HAD been torturous. Hank was running on too little sleep as he worked to solve the problems plaguing Gingerbread Inn, and keep his dream woman and her family safe.

After he'd found the shovel placed just right to trip someone coming out of the house, Hank had known the situation was more serious than he'd anticipated. This wasn't just a few weird accidents. Someone was out to cause injury.

He'd spent the last couple of days since the display room rebuild on the phone with social workers and hospital personnel. He'd found Jimmy's caretaker and they would be here later tonight. He had also found out some other news. News he was loath to share with Bella, though he knew she'd want to know.

Right now, however, despite how tired he was, he was in absolute heaven. When he'd walked in the front door, it had been as if an angel was standing there waiting for him. Her dress showed off every slim curve she had, but still came down to just below her knee. The heels she was wearing made her legs look much longer, and it created a long, smooth body line that had him feeling hot at the collar.

Her greeting, however, is what had put him over the edge. Forty-eight hours without seeing or touching her was too long, as evidenced by the fact that he couldn't seem to get enough.

His arms wound around her back and he shifted her just right so he could straighten up, pulling her up with him. After a slight squeak of surprise, Bella wound her arms around his neck and continued kissing him with reckless abandon.

Her eagerness and returned affection did absolutely nothing for his self-control. Most of their time together had been in working on the case, and it was wearing on him. He wanted to do much more than share cocoa and a few notes with her. He wanted time to snuggle in front of a movie. He wanted to hold her hand and walk through the park. He wanted to sit by her at church, with his arm around her shoulders, showing everyone that she was with him.

He wanted way more than he was going to get by the new year when she went back to her old job.

After who knew how long, but still wasn't long enough, Hank forced himself to pull back. His breathing was heavy and his pulse erratic, yet he still didn't feel satisfied. He wasn't sure he ever would with the sassy Bella.

"I think you should always greet me that way," Bella whispered hoarsely. Her lips were slightly swollen from his attack and her lip gloss had disappeared.

Hank licked his own lips and realized most of it was on him. *Yeah...that's going to look good at the party.* "Only if you promise to keep calling me delicious."

Bella laughed and kicked her legs. "I'm going to lose my shoes if you don't put me down."

Hank grinned and slowly lowered her to her feet. He kept a hold of her for a moment to make sure she had her balance before completely letting go. His desire for her was growing insatiable. If he didn't back away now, he might not do it at all. "Considering the fact that those shoes are a hazard to mankind, I don't know that that would be much of a travesty."

She scowled at him and smoothed her dress over her midsection. "These shoes are the only reason I'm not trampled on by all you jolly green giants running around." She sniffed and put her nose in the air with feigned snobbery.

Hank grinned and took her hand in his. "Lead me to the display room, my beautiful woman. I'm starving and you promised me cinnamon and sugar."

"Cinnamon and sugar that Emory baked to perfection," Bella corrected, walking him through the mansion.

"That's right. Apparently I don't want the stuff you baked."

She elbowed him in the side, but was smiling. "I'd argue the point, but really...you don't want anything I bake. I'm awful."

He wrapped his arm around her shoulders and tucked her into his side. "Good thing you have other gifts to recommend you."

"One of these days when the case is solved, I'll have you sit down and tell them all to me," she quipped, making Hank laugh harder.

"That's my girl," he whispered, kissing the top of her head as they entered the festival room. His eyes roamed. "We did a pretty good job in here. No one should be able to tell it was completely remade."

"We did," Bella said, the satisfaction clear in her voice. "It's like a fairy world." She smiled up at him. "Speaking of fairies, you have *got* to see what Antony made for his entry. It's otherworldly."

"Whoa...even better than Emory's house?" Hank had seen Emory's display several times during its creation since he had spent so much time at the inn. She had more talent in her little finger than most people did in their whole body. Her house looked like a Norman Rockwell painting. The intricacy of her work still made him shake his head.

Bella looked around and leaned in, her hand covering her mouth. "It is. But don't tell Emory I said that. She's amazing, but Antony's is..." Bella made a face. "I don't think there are words to describe it."

"This I have to see," Hank murmured. "Show the way."

Bella tugged him along. "Right over there." She pointed to the curve of the display.

Hank felt his eyes widen. "Holy cow." The gingerbread tree looked like something out of Narnia. Bella was right, there were no words to describe his abilities.

"You know what this means, don't you?" she whispered.

"What?" Hank looked down into her bright eyes. The low lights in the room highlighted the shadows and contours of her face and he wished they were alone right now. *This group might be a blessing in disguise,* he scolded himself. *If I was alone with Bella, I have to admit I'd be hard-pressed to keep my actions appropriate.*

"If Antony and Emory get married, they're going to have like...super babies," Bella said, shaking her head. "Can you imagine the artistic talent those two would create? I'll bet one of their kids will be an Iron Chef."

Hank barked out a laugh, then forced himself into submission when several people looked his way.

"I can't take you anywhere," Bella huffed, putting her hands on her hips. "It wasn't funny. I was serious."

"And that's exactly why it was funny."

She grinned and winked. "Maybe I should quit my day job."

"If that's what you want," Hank said, his attention straying to the table of baked goods. "But not before you feed me."

"Women haven't done that since they were liberated," Bella stated firmly. "But I'll take you to the table so you can feed yourself."

"So mean."

She laughed. "Get used to it, Sherlock."

Hank followed her to the table, feeling lighter and happier than he had in ages. He had no idea how his life had become so much more than it was before. Falling in love had somehow eased the burdens he carried, made work less satisfying, and made his off time something to look forward to.

He watched her fill a plate with goodies. Her smile and laughter resonated deep inside him and he had to bite his tongue from sharing his feelings. He had high hopes that she felt the same way he did, but he couldn't tell her. Not yet. He couldn't share all that was inside him until he had finished saving Gingerbread Inn and her family.

Only when that was no longer hanging over his head would he be free to concentrate on beautiful Bella and take their relationship to the next level. But the mystery would be able to wait until tomorrow. Tonight, he had every intention of enjoying the night with her by his side and letting the unknown hold for just a little bit longer.

CHAPTER 13

Bella backed away from the tight crowd, still clapping for the winners she had just announced for the gingerbread competition. She was thrilled for her cousin, even if Emory hadn't quite achieved her goal. With the level of competition this year, it was amazing to win anything at all.

Bella smirked as she saw Mrs. Pearson huff out of the inn. The local, older woman had been beyond rude and had even tried to sabotage Antony and Emory. "She's lucky she didn't get kicked out of the competition altogether," Bella grumbled.

She squeaked when arms slid around her waist from behind. "What are you complaining about now?" Henry's deep voice caressed her ear.

A shiver ran up Bella's spine and she spun to face him. There was something different about Henry tonight. He seemed...happier than usual. Like a burden had been lifted from his shoulders or something heavy was gone from his life. Reaching up, Bella ran her fingers through his hair. "Nothing," she said softly. "I'm just happy for Emory and Tony."

Henry nodded, his eyes never wavering in their intensity. "They both did a wonderful job."

"They did," she agreed, resting her hands against his chest. "So...what are your plans for the rest of the evening?"

Henry made a thinking face and contemplated for a moment before looking back at her. "I don't know for sure, but I'm hoping it involves you."

Bella grinned. "If only you're that lucky."

He smirked. "I make my own luck."

Bella whistled quietly. "Wow. That's pretty bold."

He tilted his head and gave her a hard look. "No more than you."

Bella laughed and patted his strong pectoral muscle. "Guilty."

Henry brought his head up and looked around the room, then came back to her. "Want to get out of here? Spend a little time together?"

She narrowed her gaze. "What about the case?"

Henry leaned down very slowly, his look purely seductive. "No case tonight. It's Christmas Eve. There'll be time enough for that later."

"Hmmm..." Bella tried to hold back her excitement and act coy. She loved working on the case with Henry, but their relationship had only revolved around it. She knew she had fallen hard and fast for him, and she was hungry for time without weird accidents hanging over their heads. "I might be persuaded."

He pulled her in tighter and kissed her temple, leaving his lips against her skin as he spoke. "What can I do to convince you this is a good idea?"

Nothing. I already believe you! she wanted to shout. Her pulse was racing as if she'd run a marathon and the butterflies in her stomach were doing loop de loops. Her hands clenched the front of his shirt, giving away her anticipation. "Promise me a kiss or two, and I'll take you to somewhere more private."

"No promise necessary," he murmured. "That was already guaranteed."

"Cocky." She tsked her tongue.

"Confident," he shot back.

"Both," she said with a smile, leaning back to look him in the eye. "Come on. Let's grab a plate of cookies, then we can turn on a movie or something. We have a space that's off-limits to guests."

"On it." Henry pulled away from her and Bella felt unexpectedly cold. She rubbed her upper arm and headed to the doorway to wait for her detective. A goofy smile played on her lips and she did nothing to hide it. She was so ready to be done with everything at the inn and just enjoy his company for a while. Bella wanted to know if his feelings matched her own and whether or not she should stick around after the new year.

As she turned to see him walking her way, a plate in hand, and him staring at her in that smoldering way of his, she felt pretty confident her feelings were not unreciprocated. "Ready?" she asked, clearing her throat when the sound came out far more breathless than she'd meant it to.

"Ready," he said firmly.

Bella paused for a split second, feeling like there was a hidden meaning in his words, but instead of pressing the matter, she took his free hand and led him out of the room and down the hall.

When the mansion had been turned into a bed and breakfast, a large sitting room at the far end of the hallway had been turned into a family room of sorts. A television, fireplace, and several couches were scattered around the area, making for a cozy place to get away from the stress of hospitality work.

"You can set the cookies there," Bella said, pointing to the coffee table. "Now...what would you like to watch?" She turned when he didn't answer and felt an immediate flush at his look.

"Are you on the agenda?" Henry asked, setting the plate down without breaking eye contact.

Bella swallowed hard. This was one of those times when she should have been reveling in her power, but instead she found herself unequal to the task. Henry held all the cards here. She wanted to be coy and cute, teasing and fun, but instead, she was a quivering mass of nerves and raging hormones.

This man had the ability to break her heart, though she hoped he wouldn't. But to see his attention so singularly focused on her felt empowering and terrifying at the same time.

He stepped into her personal bubble and looked down. "You didn't answer the question." His voice was low and husky.

"I..." She began to shake. "I don't know what to say."

Slowly, his hands landed on her waist and pushed her back into the wall. "Are you scared, my beautiful Bella?" he asked, lowering his head to leave a feather-light kiss on her cheekbone.

She could barely breathe at his tender touch. "Y-yes," she managed to squeak out. Her hands gripped his forearms, placed on either side of her head.

"Why?" He slid his lips along her skin and continued to leave the lightest of kisses every couple inches.

"Because I'm afraid you'll break me," she answered.

Henry paused for a second before continuing his perusal of her skin. "If I broke you, sweet Belle, it would break me as well." His arms came off the wall to gather her against his chest. "You've done something to me no other woman has and I'm ready to take that leap of faith." His lips were just under her ear. "Will you take it with me?"

She was going to melt into a tiny puddle at his feet if he didn't kiss her mouth soon. The anticipation he'd been building was coming to a head and Bella found her knees shaking with the force of it. But his words were the most beautiful part of his attention and her heart soared with the knowledge that she wasn't alone. "Always," she breathed before turning her head and capturing his mouth.

She may have started the kiss, but it only took Henry half a second to take over, and it was all Bella could do to hang on and stay upright.

THIS. I WANT THIS. Forever. Hank knew he should pull back and let the poor woman breathe, but who had that kind of self-control? Even the crick in his neck from leaning down so far couldn't seem to break through the haze of holding the woman he loved in his arms.

He'd basically confessed it all to her, though he still needed to say the words out loud, and had been elated when she'd made it clear she felt the same way. This wasn't about the banter, the flirting, or even the attraction they had immediately shared. This was about two people who were meant to be together.

He chuckled as he thought about a lifetime of keeping her out of trouble or chasing her when she got some crazy idea in her head. The thought was both wearisome and exciting, but the laughter broke his connection to her.

"What in the world are you laughing about?" she asked, panting heavily from their kissing.

"Sorry," Hank said, kissing her forehead quickly. "Just had a funny thought."

"That was more important than kissing me?" she pouted.

"It was about you."

"But you were laughing." Bella pursed her swollen lips and Hank shook his head. Why in the world was he arguing with her when he could be kissing her?

"Forget it," he whispered, bringing his mouth back to hers. His distraction only worked for a moment before she pulled free.

"I can't," she said, pressing against his chest.

Hank frowned. "Can't what?"

"Stop thinking about it."

"What?"

Bella gave him a look. "The laughing."

"Are you serious?" The thick electricity in the air was slowly waning as she argued with him.

Bella walked her fingers up his chest and the air crackled again. "I want to know why my kisses made you laugh."

Hank glanced heavenward and shook his head. "It wasn't your kiss that made me laugh. It was a different thought." He gave her a peck, then another one, hoping to get her back on track. "Your kisses make me lose my mind," he said between quick touches.

"Not enough that you can't think funny thoughts," she retorted.

Hank hung his head back and groaned. "Bella!"

"Shhh!" She put a finger to his lips.

"What are you—"

Bella's fierce glare caused him to snap his mouth shut. As soon as he did, he realized a strange noise was coming from...the walls.

Hank stiffened, then let go of Bella and slowly crept across the hardwood, trying not to make any noise. A scuffling sound was coming from the corner of the room, as if a mouse or other creature was inside the wall. However, the noise was much too large for a normal rodent.

Hank put his ear to the wall and his eyebrows shot up. Someone was muttering. *Crap,* he thought. *The perp is in the tunnels.* A smaller head went on the wall as well and Hank scowled.

Grabbing Bella's hand, he drug her to the center of the room. "I want you to go out into the party and grab Sheriff Davidson," Hank whispered, pushing her toward the door.

"Are you kidding me?" she whispered back incredulously. "Whoever's been sabotaging the inn is right there," her arm went to the wall, "and you think I'm going to hightail it away?"

"Yes," Hank declared, putting his foot down. "I'm going to need the police if we're going to catch the guy." *And I want you somewhere safe while I chase them down.* "Now hurry before they get away."

"Not happening."

"Bella. Go."

"No."

Heaven save me from stubborn women. Hank's anxiety for her was growing by the second. He couldn't stand the thought of her being in danger, and with each moment that passed, the chances of her either getting hurt or the intruder getting away grew exponentially. "Bella," he said in a soft tone, hoping to convince her to see things his way. "Please. For me. I'm asking you to go get help."

His plea did nothing. "I'm not leaving." She folded her arms over her chest.

Hank opened his mouth, but the noise from the walls grew louder and Bella's jaw dropped.

"The closet," she mouthed, pointing behind him.

Hank spun and realized the intruder was entering the room through a small closet in the far corner. Several things in the closet fell over and cursing could be heard. Grabbing Bella, Hank leapt over the couch and took her to the ground behind the furniture. If they were lucky, the intruder wouldn't see them in this spot.

She groaned when his body landed on top of hers and he had a moment's worry that his size would crush her.

"Are you okay?" Hank whispered against her ear.

"You're huge, you know that?" she whispered back, just as inaudibly.

He bit back a grin and laughter. Now was not the time for humor. "I know and I'm sorry." He put his elbows down and tried to keep his weight from smothering her, only to duck his head even more as he heard someone stomping across the hardwood. His eyes went down to Bella's wide ones. Hank put a finger to his lips and she nodded jerkily.

"Can't believe I have to do this again," a low voice grumbled. "Why can't someone just get hurt already?" The door to the room opened, then slammed shut quickly.

Hank jumped to his feet.

"Why in the world didn't you just wait for him to come out and then catch him?" Bella asked, struggling to her feet. Her heels and dress weren't exactly the right outfit for their escape that evening.

"Because I have no idea who this guy is," Hank explained, walking quickly to the door. "It could have been some teenager using the tunnels to get into the party."

"But?"

"But by letting them go I can now follow, and if they do something untoward, I'll have evidence to take them down."

"Great." Bella pulled off her high heels and dropped them, then hurried to his side. "Let's go." She rubbed her hands together.

"You're not coming with me," Hank said forcefully, keeping his face neutral. "You stay here and then in two minutes, go get the sheriff." He put up a hand to stop her argument. "Stop, Bella. You promised in the beginning you'd listen to the professional. Now's that time." He kissed her cheek. "I'll see you soon and we'll finish that conversation from earlier." Without another word, he peeked out the doorway and darted out. It was time to catch a criminal.

CHAPTER 14

Bella pinched her lips together in frustration. "If he thinks I'm going to run and hide while he has all the fun, he's got another thing coming." Grabbing her cell phone from her bra, she texted her grandmother, hoping Grandma Claire had her phone on her.

Bring the sheriff. We found the saboteur.

Stuffing the phone away, she peeked out into the hallway. Bella bit her lip. Hank and the other guy were gone, but that didn't mean it was all over yet. "But where can I catch up with them?" Her eyes drifted to the closet the guy had come through. "Perfect."

Not bothering to grab her shoes, knowing they would slow her down, Bella slid across the floor in her stockings and opened the closet door. "Come on, come oooon," she begged as she searched the walls. A broom and vacuum had been pushed to the side and Bella searched the wall carefully, but found nothing. "Where is it?" She finally bent her knees and looked at the bottom of the wall. "Aha!"

A thin line drug through the dust and Bella followed it until she was able to pull at the edge of the door. "Duh," she muttered to herself when she realized the door was only waist high. "I forgot Enoch said the bedroom entrance was the same way." She blew out a long breath. "I guess that's one way of keeping it from being seen."

She got on her hands and knees and started to crawl into the door, when she heard footsteps on the hardwood.

"Bella?"

She grit her teeth. "Of all the times for Henry to come back." Pretending she didn't hear him, Bella hurried to crawl through the entrance. She knew he would stop her if he caught her.

"BELLA!" he shouted, his footsteps loud on the floor as he came her way.

With a squeal, she scrambled into the hidden passage, stumbling to her feet when she made it inside and slamming the door shut.

"Bella..." Henry warned. He pounded on the closed opening. "What are you doing? Come back out here!"

"I'm going to see if I can figure out where they were coming from," she snapped, brushing off her dirty knees. Pulling her cell phone back out, she turned on the flashlight feature.

"Sweetheart, you're going to get hurt. Come out here, please." The please was said through a tight jaw and Bella knew she was pushing things with him.

"Henry, you know I love you, but I won't let you lock me away and never get in on the action."

"I have no intention of locking you away, but we still don't know what we're dealing with here." Henry grunted and Bella realized he was trying to get through the opening, but the door must have jammed when she slammed it. Who knew how warped the old wood was.

He sighed. "Just come out. I lost track of them and could use your help at the party. You might see who looks out of place."

Bella paused. His plan did sound good. She might know who didn't belong, or at least who hadn't been there earlier, but she was afraid if she came out, he would force her to stay back when the excitement came.

"Bella, please," he begged, his voice sounding defeated. "It would kill me if you got hurt."

The sound of muffled footsteps came from somewhere farther in the house, and both she and Henry froze.

"He's in here," she whispered, sweat breaking out on her forehead. For the first time since this all started, she was starting to feel real fear. Henry was right. They had no idea who they were dealing with, only that someone wanted to sabotage the inn. And she was standing right now in a passage that Henry couldn't get into in order to help her if there was trouble.

NO! she screamed internally. *You want to be a crime journalist? Then you need to be willing to push past the fear. Go for the story. Catch the bad guy. That all happens right now.*

More footsteps went over their heads and dust rained onto her hair. "He's above us," she whispered. "You go through the house, and I'll go this way."

"Bella, no! Bella!"

Hank's voice was loud in the dark passageway she was currently navigating, and the frightened part of her wanted to go back and let him hold her hand and tell her it would all be all right. But the other part of her was desperate for a chance to prove herself. She needed this. She needed to finally succeed in her field and show the news stations that she wasn't just a cute face, but a serious writer.

She heard Henry curse and then run across the family room and out the door. Sending a quick prayer for his safety, she continued to move through the skinny hallway. The footsteps overhead were moving faster and Bella was having a hard time keeping up.

Her phone buzzed in her hand, nearly startling Bella out of her skin. Glancing at the notifications, she realized Henry was texting her like crazy. With a huff, she turned off the sound and continued onward. She would deal with him later.

It took another thirty seconds before she froze in place. The steps from above were moving decidedly closer and Bella realized the person was coming down a set of steps in her direction.

"Crud. Crud. Crud." She shone her light around, trying to find a place to hide, but the hallway had no exits or entrances. She spun in a circle, wincing when the old wooden boards scraped against her bare feet.

The footsteps were even closer, sounding ominous in their arrival.

Shutting off her flashlight, Bella pressed herself against the wall, hoping and praying with everything in her that the person would either change direction or manage to slip by without noticing her in the dark. Her hand slid farther back than her body and she realized there was a deep spot between beams. Squishing herself to be as tiny as possible, Bella slid between the two-by-fours and tried to be invisible.

Dust tickled her nose and she had no idea what was crawling over her foot, but nothing was as important as staying silent.

Biting her tongue until she bled, Bella held in the scream that wanted to erupt. Between the disgusting creatures and cobwebs and the anticipation of being caught, she felt as if her body were completely out of control.

A flashlight beam appeared on the boards just in front of her and Bella sucked in a breath, flattening herself as far back as she could. The light bounced slightly, moving farther down the floorboards as the person holding the light drew closer.

A dark shadow passed just in front of her and Bella squeezed her eyes shut. The footsteps didn't seem to falter as they walked by her, taking the flashlight with her. She started to let out her breath, only to stop breathing again when the feet paused.

Please, no. Keep moving. Keep moving.

To her relief, they resumed pace and eventually walked around a corner.

Bella stiffened her knees and wedged herself free of the boards. Taking a fortifying breath, she began to tiptoe after the intruder when a light blinded her, causing Bella to gasp.

"What do we have here?" a low voice asked with a dark chuckle.

HANK USED EVERY CURSE word in his vocabulary as he searched for Sheriff Davidson at the party. Then he used them again when the man wasn't in the room.

"Where the heck is he?" he snapped. Rushing from the room, he headed into the kitchen and skidded to a stop. "Uh...Sheriff?"

"What?" Sheriff Davidson let go of Claire Simmons and cleared his throat, pushing a hand through his hair. "I'm sorry, son, but this was—"

Hank held a hand up. While it was interesting to have found the sheriff kissing Bella's grandmother, it wasn't his main concern at the moment. "We've got a problem."

The sheriff cleared his throat again. "Sorry, Claire," he muttered. "I have to go."

"Wait!" Claire cried as the men started to move. Her hands were trembling as she held her phone. "Bella texted, said you found the saboteur?" Claire's blue eyes, so like Bella's, met Hank's. "But I'm guessing from the way you stormed in here that's not quite true."

"Someone was in the walls," Hank explained. "I wanted Bella to come get the sheriff while I followed him."

"Then where is she?"

Hank blew out a breath and rubbed the back of his neck. "She went into the walls to try and figure out where the guy had disappeared to."

Claire groaned and swayed slightly, causing Bill to rush to her side. "Claire, honey, let's get you a seat."

"I love that girl, but she's gonna get herself killed!" Claire cried.

Hank shook his head. "While I'm not happy with her, we're not dealing with a murderer here," he said matter of factly.

Claire gave him a hard look. "You think someone like this wouldn't grow desperate if they were worried about being exposed?"

Hank swallowed the rock in his throat. "I don't know," he admitted. His fear for Bella was already driving him crazy. He could barely concentrate on the situation since all of his instincts were screaming for him to break open that small opening and go after her.

A terrified scream sounded and Hank froze for a second. "Bella," he breathed.

"Dang girl must have found him," Bill shouted as he rushed after Hank.

The sound had come from deep inside the house and Hank rushed to that wing, but found nothing amiss. He pounded against the walls of the hallway. "Where is she?"

Some scuffling sounded and Hank followed it, Sheriff Davidson right on his heels.

The sounds were moving slowly and Hank realized they were moving toward an outside entrance to the home. His eyes went to the door at the end of the hallway, the one that led to the side of the house with the garden shed.

Without telling Bill what he was doing, Hank ran for the door and burst outside. His breath came in great gusts of air, turning into white fog in the chilly weather. "Where was that entrance?" he muttered to himself, walking along the side of the house.

Before he could go too far, Hank stilled. A small door on the corner of the house was starting to swing open. Hank glanced at his hands and cursed again. He didn't have anything with him in order to fight. He'd left everything home with the intent of spending time with Bella.

"I've got your back," Bill whispered, pulling a gun from the back of his belt.

Hank nodded, grateful the sheriff had come armed, and kept his eyes on the door. A slim leg came out first and Hank's heart nearly pounded out of his ribcage.

"Let me go!" Bella cried, though the sound was muffled against someone's hand. "So help me, George, if you don't let me go I'm going to—"

George? As in the cousin?

"OW!" bellowed the man's voice. "You'll pay for that," he hissed as he pushed Bella outside, holding her against his chest. "Stupid cousins. Always taking, never sharing." George's voice trailed off and he froze when he realized he had an audience.

"Let her go, son," Sheriff Davidson said, holding his gun up and stepping up to Hank's side.

Hank clenched his fists. He wanted Bella away from the maniac, but was afraid the man would do something to hurt her before all was said and done.

As far as Hank could tell, the man didn't have anything else on him except for the flashlight in his hand. But it was large and would definitely give someone a concussion if used properly.

Hank almost deflated in relief when George dropped his flashlight.

"That's right," Bill began. "Just—"

George fumbled in his back pocket and brought something to Bella's throat. "Back off!" he shouted, stepping backward. "Or I'll cut her throat."

Hank's heart almost stopped. *No.* George had a razor blade in his hand and it was against his Bella. Hank's worst nightmare was about to come true. He put his hands in the air. "Let's talk this out," he said, his voice shakier than he wanted it to be. Usually he was the picture of calm during a hostage take-down, but right now, he was about to lose his mind. "No one needs to get hurt."

George barked out a wild laugh. "Oh, really? Just like my family didn't need to get hurt by being left out of the will?"

"Are you still going on about the inn, you idiot?" Bella shouted. She wiggled against his hold, but stilled when the blade came up tighter against her neck. "Your grandmother is to blame," she wheezed. "She wanted nothing to do with the family."

"Only because she didn't know how much this place was worth," George spat, his face growing more and more determined. "She cut us all out. We could be sitting pretty if she'd left us the inheritance we deserved. Instead, she agreed to let it go. Hurting her entire posterity in the process."

"So you've been what?" Hank asked, slowly taking a step forward. "You're already suing for access. What else have you been doing?"

George snickered. "You haven't figured it out yet? The big bad detective still hasn't put all the pieces together, huh?"

"Don't you talk about him that way," Bella growled.

"Shut up," George said harshly, using the hand holding her neck to cut into her windpipe.

Hank felt his heart skip a beat when Bella began to turn red. He really wanted to pummel this guy, but first he had to get Bella away. He took another step forward, but George backed up. "I think you've been busy," Hank said, forcing his voice to obey and stay calm. "I think you've been causing accidents around here, or at least hoping to."

"Oh, yeah?" George asked. "And just why would I do that?"

"Because you're trying to make Claire look incompetent," Hank guessed, trying another step forward. The lawsuit had been on his mind lately, the more he mused over Claire's accident and the nature of the problems still occurring at the inn. "You're trying to show the courts she's neglectful, and the only way to do that is for someone to get hurt on the property. That's why you left all the tools lying around, and towels on the floor. Not to mention the ice on the sidewalk."

Hank met Bella's surprised eyes as the pieces fell into place. He was glad to see she was breathing again, but when a determined look came into her eyes, he grew scared all over again.

George was talking again, but Hank couldn't drag his eyes from Bella.

"You can't prove I did any of those things," George argued. "Not to mention, none of them are illegal."

"Maybe not, but slashing tires means we can bring you downtown for destruction of property," Hank continued. He'd noticed several flats when he was trying to follow George earlier, and with the razor blade in his hand, Hank was throwing out another guess. He stiffened when Bella mouthed something to him.

"I love you," she said, her lips over-exaggerating the words.

Hank didn't know what she was planning, but it wasn't going to be good. He started to shake his head, but it was too late.

Slamming her head backwards, Bella crushed George's nose with an awful crunching sound.

He howled and jerked away from her, but Bella wasn't done yet. She elbowed his sternum, causing him to bend over wheezing. Spinning on her bare feet, Bella kicked George right between the legs, which proved to be the final blow for the man.

Whimpering and crying, he fell to his knees, then onto his side, leaving Bella free to run to Hank's arms.

He opened them and welcomed her in, nearly crying in relief that she was alive and well. "I think I'm going to kill you myself," he muttered into her hair.

"Ha! Just try and I'll show you what I showed George," Bella shot back, but Hank could feel her trembling against him.

She might still be able to talk big game, but he could tell the situation had frightened her more than she was letting on.

CHAPTER 15

Bella couldn't seem to get her body to stop shaking. She was freezing, weak from her adrenaline rush, and scared out of her mind.

"If you ever pull something like that again, I'll make you cook me dinner every night when we're married," Henry whispered hoarsely as he held her tightly. His strong arms were nearly choking her, but Bella didn't care. They were the only thing still holding her upright.

"What do you mean, when we're married?" she asked, latching onto the words that she hadn't heard before. Bella leaned back to confront him, but Henry wasn't ready to talk yet.

His mouth met hers in a voracious kiss that took the very air from her lungs. Rather than pull back and tease him, she reached up and wrapped her arms around his neck, holding on for dear life.

The tension and anxiety of the situation was making her emotions more volatile than usual, and she found she couldn't quench her thirst for the handsome detective.

His hand slid along her jaw, going into her hair, and Bella winced as he passed a sore spot.

Henry jerked away from her, gasping. "What? Are you hurt?"

Bella shook her head. "No. Sorry. But I'm probably going to have a few—"

Henry's large hand grabbed her head and turned it sideways. "Bella...you're bleeding!"

"What?"

"We need an ambulance," Henry continued, his fear palpable and his eyes wild. "Bill! We need an ambulance!"

Bella fingered the cut on her jawline and frowned. It didn't feel that bad, though by the wetness, she could tell there was blood.

Sheriff Davidson walked their way, holding up a hand. "Hang in there, Hank. If you'll just calm down, I think you'll find everything's going to be okay."

"She's bleeding," Henry growled.

Sheriff Davidson nodded. "Yes. His razor gave her a little cut. Wipe it off with hydrogen peroxide and slap a Band-Aid on it, and she'll be good as new."

"Slap a—?" Henry shook his head and started to step away from her.

"Henry. Henry!" Bella shouted to get his attention. She cupped his face. "You need to calm down. I'm okay. Yes, the situation with my rat of a cousin was frightening, but I'm here. I'm fine. You were magnificent as you unriddled the whole thing, and now you've told me we're getting married." She gave him a little shake. "Get a hold of yourself."

"We're getting married?" he asked in a softer tone, his tense muscles slowly easing.

"You said so yourself," she said sweetly, bringing his face down for a quick peck. "But you also said you wanted me to cook, so I think you have a death wish."

Henry closed his eyes and huffed a quiet laugh. "We can work out anything you want as long as you don't scare me like that again."

Bella snuggled into his chest. "I'll think about it," she hedged. "Unless it comes to winning my Pulitzer. On that story, I won't budge. Sorry." She shrugged a dainty shoulder, knowing her nonchalance would drive him crazy.

Seeing Henry so riled up on her behalf was a better answer to her declaration of love than anything he could have said. She could see it in his eyes the whole time he was speaking. Nothing had scared him about the situation until Bella had been in danger.

Truth be told, it had frightened her as well, but she had tried not to let it show. All of Henry's warnings had been running through her head while George held her in his grip. She squeezed her eyes shut and clutched at Henry.

If she hadn't been caught so unawares, she would never have let that weasel take her. But in the dark, with his flashlight keeping her blind, she hadn't had a chance to react before he'd squeezed her throat.

She'd tried to make noise as they had walked through the walls to the outside entrance, hoping to draw attention to them, and it must have worked, since Henry and Sheriff Davidson were waiting. A fact which Bella would be forever grateful for.

But when George began to taunt and say horrible things about the family, Bella couldn't stand it any longer. Someone had to take that bozo down, and she was in the best position to do it.

Blue and red lights flashed over the yard and everyone turned to see the police and an ambulance pulling up.

Henry looked down at her, running his thumb along her jaw. "Should we have you checked out?" he asked, his eyes roaming her face as if to memorize it.

Bella shook her head. "No. I'm fine." She shivered. "Cold, exhausted, angry, excited, a little bit hungry...but fine."

Henry shook his head and chuckled. "That was quite a descriptive list, love."

She grinned. "I'm full of words. Just ask my editors."

Henry pulled her in for a tight hug. "I'm not happy about it, but I'm going to have to work with the police before I can fix everything on your list."

She perked up. "I'm coming too."

Henry shook his head. "Not a chance. You need to go inside and warm up. In fact..." Without warning, he swept her into his arms.

"What are you doing?" Bella cried, kicking her legs. "Put me down!"

"Nope. You already ran away once. I don't trust you not to do it again." Henry walked to the open side door and marched down the hallway, still carrying her. "Claire!" he hollered.

"Don't you dare sic Grandma on me," Bella warned. She knew all too well that if Grandma got a hold of her, she would never make it down to the police station for the inside scoop.

Henry's eyes twinkled with triumph when Grandma Claire met them at the end of the hallway.

"Oh, my dear, sweet girl," she sobbed. "You're okay!"

"You'll pay for this," she whispered in his ear, then gave him a saccharine sweet smile.

"She loves you," Henry whispered back, pulling her into his chest once her feet were on the ground. "Give her some slack."

Grandma limped over and wrapped Bella in a tight, familiar hug.

With a sigh, Bella let herself relax and enjoy the comfort that was being offered. Maybe going to the police station could wait.

Henry started walking down the hallway, the way he had come in. "Oh...by the way. I caught Sheriff Davidson smooching your grandma in the kitchen!" he called over his shoulder just before slipping out the door.

Bella's jaw went slack and she pulled back to look Grandma Claire in the face. "You what?"

"Traitor!" Grandma hollered after Henry before meeting Bella's gaze. "What?" she demanded, putting her hands on her round hips. "You can only let a handsome man run around for so long before a girl has to do something about it!"

HENRY CHUCKLED AS HE shut the outside door. Between Bella's rescue and Claire's revelation, he knew the women wouldn't be coming up for air any time soon.

"You're a sneaky jerk," Bill whispered in an aside as he watched the police lead a limping and still crying George to their vehicle.

Henry shrugged. Bill had obviously heard Henry's accusation as he'd left the house. "Did you really think it would stay a secret? Enoch told me he's been watching you two dance around each other for years."

Sheriff Davidson hitched up his pants and cleared his throat. "Well, with all you young ones running around kissing every other second, it leaves ideas in a man's head."

Henry clapped his friend on the shoulder. "Good for you. But don't expect me to call you Grandpa when all is said and done."

The good sheriff stammered a bit before shaking his head. "We're getting ahead of ourselves and we have a job to do." Raising his hand, he walked out to one of the police officers to talk to them.

Hank watched him go with a smile, which quickly turned to a frown. He glanced back at the house. Every part of him wanted to be inside with Bella. Holding her and making sure she was okay. He wanted to listen to her side of the story, know what happened, and get this all figured out. Eventually she would need to give a statement to the police, but right now, he wanted her safe and well. And that meant inside with her family.

He stood and watched the commotion for a few more minutes when an officer approached. "I just spoke to Ms. Woods," he said, looking down at his notebook. "Do you want me to bring her in? Or is a written statement enough?"

Henry wanted to growl. He hadn't wanted Bella disturbed at all, but then he sighed. His heart was overruling what he needed to do as a detective, and that wasn't how it should be. "Written is enough," he huffed. "If we need more from her, we know where to find her."

The officer nodded and put the notebook in their pocket. "Looks like we've about got it." They turned to the driveway. "Except we're going to have a bunch of angry people when they discover their tires are all slashed."

Hank sighed and pinched the bridge of his nose. "Have a few officers wait around and help those who need help changing their tires. For anyone without a spare, offer them a ride home until it can all be figured out." He looked up. "Do we know how many were sliced?"

"Best we can tell, there were six cars," the officer stated, putting his hands on his hips.

Hank nodded. "Not as bad as I feared," he murmured.

"But enough to cause a riot."

Henry snorted. "True enough."

"Anything else?"

Hank shook his head. "No. Get that idiot downtown, then Bill—Sheriff Davidson—and I will give our own statements before he's booked." He jerked his chin toward the car with George sitting in the back.

The officer nodded and headed off, leaving Hank with his thoughts. He forced his feet into action, walking to where he'd parked. *The sooner you get this taken care of, the more time you can spend with Bella. Come on. Let's get it done.*

Those words got him through the next twelve hours as he stayed awake all night at the station, helping piece together the disasters that had happened at Gingerbread Inn.

As he walked outside, Hank put a hand to his eyes, the sun bright but offering no warmth on the crisp Christmas morning.

"You going to bed?" Bill asked with a yawn.

Hank thought about it, then shook his head. "No. I don't think I can rest until I check on her."

"Claire says she's doing fine," the sheriff offered.

Hank nodded. "Thanks, but I'd like to see for myself."

Bill slapped him on the back. "Merry Christmas, son."

"That's grandson to you!" Hank called out, laughing quietly when Bill waved an agitated hand at him.

Hank was exhausted. He'd been up for too long and the adrenaline from the night before had long since slipped away. But he knew his mind would never rest unless he got to see Bella in person.

Tightening his grip on his keys, he climbed into his car and headed back up the hill. It only took minutes to arrive. The mansion looked much less busy than last night. The grounds were misty with a low-lying fog and the house was still lit up with Christmas lights. A large wreath on the door offered a much-needed splash of color that beckoned him inside.

"Maybe Emory has something on the stove that'll keep me awake," he muttered to himself as he climbed the front steps. His legs felt like lead and his head could barely think clearly. He gave a sharp rap on the door and waited.

"Well, if it isn't our very own Sherlock."

Hank grinned at the petite ball of sass in front of him. She looked radiant. Her skin practically glowed and her eyes were warm and welcoming. She'd obviously recovered from her experience the night before. Her toes, as usual, were tapping out a rhythm that no one could hear but her, and it was enough to let him know he had come to the right place. "I needed to see that you were okay."

Bella grinned and grabbed his hand, dragging him inside. "Come on, handsome. Emory has some warm cider and donuts that'll cure all your woes."

Once inside, he tugged her back into his hold. "I thought that was your job," he whispered, bringing their noses together.

"Well, duh," Bella drawled. "But even a woman like me can't cure hangry, and if we don't get you fed, I'm pretty sure that's what I'm going to have on my hands in a few minutes."

Hank frowned. "I don't get hangry."

Bella began tugging him toward the large sitting room. "Says the man who's frowning at me."

Choosing to let the argument go, since his brain couldn't keep up, Hank let himself be pulled to the couch. Exclamations and questions rang through the room at his arrival, but he couldn't process any of it. All he seemed to be able to focus on was Bella.

"Give him a moment to breathe," Bella scolded the group. She had him sit on the couch, then smiled sweetly. "I think you need a nap."

"I think I need you."

She laughed. "That can be arranged."

Hank reached out and pulled her onto his lap. "Forever?"

Bella wrapped her arms around his neck. "If that's what you want."

"It is."

"Then it's done. But I'm warning you now...I want a ring."

Hank nodded, realizing his eyes were closed. *When did that happen?* His head fell forward and landed on her shoulder. "Just as soon as I can get to the jewlers," he slurred.

Bella's warm chuckle was the last thing he heard before he slipped into sweet oblivion, dreaming of Bella in his arms, his home and his life until the end of time.

EPILOGUE

"Not happening," Henry said with a decisive snap. "I want cake, not a donut tower, or whatever the heck it is you're talking about."

Bella pursed her lips and she set her jaw. "I saw it on Pinterest and it's the only thing that I want."

Henry's eyebrows raised and his eyes went to the large solitaire on her left hand, which was currently resting on his arm as they danced. "The *only* thing?"

"What? Every girl wants a diamond," she defended.

"But not every girl gets one," he shot back.

Bella decided to change tactics. "Sherlock, honey, you don't really mind, do you? Emory will make them all from scratch for us! You love her donuts."

Henry sighed and Bella knew she had him. "You know, this would be a lot more effective if you weren't always offering your cousin's services."

Bella laughed and stepped in closer as they continued to rotate to the slow song. "Don't worry," she purred, threading her fingers through the sides of his hair. "I'll make it worth your while."

His grip on her back tightened and suddenly there wasn't an ounce of space between them. "Promise?"

"Always," she whispered, eyeing his lips.

"Hey, you two," Emory scolded. "Only the bride and groom are allowed to kiss on the dance floor."

Henry's eyes were still intense and Bella was filled with disappointment herself at the interruption. "Later," she mouthed, making Emory groan.

"Oh my word! You two are horrible!"

Bella laughed and looked over at her cousin as she danced with Tony. "Worse than you two?" Her grin widened when Emory turned pink and Tony smirked. "Or worse than Grandma and our new grandpa? I thought he was going to kiss her until she fainted when the priest gave him permission."

Henry choked on a laugh. "You're unbelievable," he stammered.

"And yet you love me anyway."

Henry smiled brilliantly. "Yes...yes, I do. But that doesn't mean you don't drive me nuts sometimes."

Bella scowled as Emory and Tony snickered. "Oh yeah?" she began. "Well you—"

"Excuse us, will you?" Henry said to the other couple. Stepping out of the dance, he took Bella's hand and led her out of the large sitting room of the mansion that had been turned back into a ballroom for the wedding.

"What's the matter? Don't want to fight in public?" Bella teased, letting herself be dragged along.

"As a matter of fact, I don't want to fight at all," he shot over his shoulder.

"Chicken," she grumbled. Their banter was her favorite part of the day. Ever since they'd gotten engaged, she couldn't seem to go twenty-four hours without teasing and kissing him. They had become her favorite things in the world.

After glancing around to make sure no one was watching, Henry pulled her across the foyer, down the hallway, and into the family room. After closing the door behind them, he pushed her up against the wall and caged her in. "Now...I think it's time we took care of Ms. Hangry."

Bella's jaw dropped. "I'm not hangry! I'm not even hungry!"

Henry's answering smirk gave her pause. When his thumb traced her jawline, she sucked in a breath, especially as he rubbed her scar several times. It was only a small, thin line, barely visible, but Henry always seemed to find it and couldn't stop touching it. "You are hungry. Just not for food."

Bella's lips pulled into a slow smile as she realized where he was going with this. She slid her hands up his chest and clasped them behind his neck. "Oh, really? Then what do you think I'm hungry for?"

"The only thing that'll satisfy you," he bragged. He gave her a slow, lingering kiss. "Your very own detective," he whispered against her lips.

"You know I hate to admit it," she said between kisses. "But you're absolutely right."

"I'm writing that down," Henry teased as he kissed her neck. "And I don't promise not to use it during a future fight."

Bella shrugged. "Don't worry. I don't fight fair either."

"Perfect," he breathed before bringing his mouth to hers.

As pleasurable shocks and emotions rushed through her, Bella forgot all about being right or wrong. All she cared about right now was enjoying her Christmas Detective as much as she could for as long as she could. They'd eventually have to go back to the wedding, but she was going to have her fill first. And nothing and no one, not even a Pulitzer Prize winning story, could pull her away.

Thank you so much for reading my story!
I certainly hope you enjoyed reading it as much as
I enjoyed writing it.
Not ready for the romance to end?
Check out all my stories at lauraannbooks.com
Or visit my Amazon Author page.

Other Books by Laura Ann

THE GINGERBREAD INN [1]

"Her Christmas Handyman"[2]

"Her Christmas Baker"[3]

"Her Christmas Detective"[4]

SAGEBRUSH RANCH

When city girls meet cowboys,
the shenanigans are epic.

Books 1-6[5]

LOCKWOOD INDUSTRIES

The Lockwood triplets started a personal security business.
Little did they know it would double as a matchmaking business!

Books 1-6[6]

OVERNIGHT BILLIONAIRE BACHELORS

Three brothers become overnight billionaires.
Will they discover that love is the real treasure?

Books 1-5[7]

IT'S ALL ABOUT THE MISTLETOE

When 6 friends brings fake dates to the Holiday Ball,
mayhem, mistletoe and love win the day!

---

1. https://www.amazon.com/gp/product/B08N4JD51P?ref_=dbs_p_mng_rwt_ser_shvlr&storeType=ebooks
2. https://www.amazon.com/dp/B08MZ3NKRM
3. https://www.amazon.com/dp/B08N4Q5KH2
4. https://www.amazon.com/dp/B08N3NKDHK
5. https://www.amazon.com/gp/product/B089YPCF6X?ref_=dbs_r_series&storeType=ebooks
6. https://www.amazon.com/gp/product/B083Z49VL3?ref_=dbs_r_series&storeType=ebooks
7. https://www.amazon.com/gp/product/B07RJZL29J?ref_=dbs_r_series&storeType=ebooks

Books 1-6[8]

MIDDLETON PREP

If you enjoy fairy tale romance,
these sweet, contemporary retellings are for you!

Books 1-9[9]

8. https://www.amazon.com/gp/product/B082F8FTHY?ref_=dbs_r_series&storeType=ebooks

9. https://www.amazon.com/gp/product/B07DYCWRQL?ref_=dbs_r_series&store-Type=ebooks

Made in United States
North Haven, CT
28 November 2021